NIGHT BOAT TO PARIS

"…a breathless tale of a British crook who was a Resistance hero during the war and now ten years later is pressured by British intelligence into heisting a high-society house party in the south of France to obtain a scrap of microfilm containing Soviet nuclear secrets… a great yarn with colorful settings from the Paris gutters to the hills of Provence, with all the action and twists and turns you could want…"
—Sam Reaves

"…an old-school, hard-boiled adventure that combines espionage, a heist, desperate criminals and ruthless shadow operators. There's plenty of action and shadow operating, but with a more sophisticated style than you get in a typical men's adventure novel… I can recommend this book to anyone who enjoys the early hardboiled spy work of authors like Donald Hamilton, Jack Higgins, Dan Marlowe and Edward Aarons."
—*GoodReads*

NIGHT BOAT TO PARIS

By Richard Jessup

Black Gat Books • Eureka California

NIGHT BOAT TO PARIS

Published by Black Gat Books
A division of Stark House Press
1315 H Street
Eureka, CA 95501, USA
griffinskye3@sbcglobal.net
www.starkhousepress.com

NIGHT BOAT TO PARIS

ISBN: 979-8-88601-091-6

Cover design by Jeff Vorzimmer, ¡caliente!design, Austin, Texas
Book design by Mark Shepard, shepgraphics.com
Cover art by George Ziel
Proofreading by Bill Kelly

First Stark House Press/Black Gat Edition: March 2024

During the ten years immediately after the war, I have been a number of things. Most notably a blackmailer, procurer, petty thief, gambler (very poor this last one) and now the owner of the Lion's Head Inn, a pub on the banks of the River Mersey in a little hamlet outside Liverpool called Rock Ferry. I achieved all this using the clever, brutal methods I learned in the war to intimidate and destroy; and in my case crime paid a handsome, if perhaps unsavory, reward.

I had been in the pub when Philip Boyler found me. He said he had been searching for several weeks tracking me down. I could understand that. Even the head of wartime intelligence would find it difficult to trail after me through the constantly changing paths of the London underworld. It was also because of Boyler that I was now standing on a street corner in Rock Ferry waiting for the cab to take me over to Manchester in time to make the five-thirty train to London. After ten years, I was once again going to do the dirty work for the proper Mr. Boyler, not to mention Queen and country; only this time at my price, not theirs.

I glanced at my watch. The cab was late. I tucked my chin down fighting the river winds. Behind me, halfway up the block, I could see the faint lights and hear the laughter from my pub. I was doing some wishful thinking about those lights and the laughter when the cab slipped out of the fog and down beside me.

"Mister Reece?"

"Yes. I must make a five-thirty appointment in St. Peter's Square. Can you manage that?" I climbed into the back and closed the door. "An extra quid if you do."

"Righto." We moved off quickly into the fog.

The night ferry for the continent left Victoria Station, London, at ten that evening. If I could be on it, I could be in Paris the next morning at nine. After looking up Tookie, I would go directly to Arles. I lit a cigarette and closed my eyes.

Another mission. And I found myself feeling and reacting as if there had been no ten-year interval. Things came to mind that I had tried to forget. Ugly things that happened after the war when patriotism had become a drag on the market and it was either return to the London docks as a timekeeper for ten quid a week or use my intelligence training in the only manner left open to me. I tried for better things, but London East End was stamped on me. The few titled and wealthy well-placed men I worked with during the war forgot. They didn't bother with the hypocrisy of avoiding me. They honestly had forgotten they ever knew me and I could read doubt in their eyes when I insisted we had known each other.

The patriot is moved to action by love of his country. But I am no longer a patriot. I was once, but no more. I pledge allegiances to the Crown, the Flag and Country, and here there is a subtle difference. The patriot places himself in his country's hands and serves anywhere, anytime. As a man who holds allegiances, I claimed reservations to Boyler that night. For one thing, I explained, I do not run off to battle for love of country. I walk, if I go at all, after private thoughts about the matter.

Boyler then made one thing clear. He wanted me for this mission. He emphasized how badly he wanted me rather than one of the young-faced, unobtrusive boys in B. I., by telling me of the fight he had had at Whitehall when my name was suggested. There had been considerable official doubt as to my integrity—considering my postwar experiences with Scotland Yard.

Boyler dismissed my objections. He handled me very nicely now that I remember it, simply telling me the facts and the nature of the mission and letting me draw my own conclusions. The Reds, Boyler told me, had been working on plans for a nuclear-supported satellite, or space station, with an old unreconstructed Nazi named Fritz Hemer doing most of the developing. Hemer had worked on the Peenemünde V-2 project and had completed hand-drawn engineer's blueprints for the space station. They had been microfilmed and the originals destroyed. Some one—Boyler did not know who—stole the microfilm and threw it on the open market in Europe. One of Boyler's men picked up the scent and made contact with a Frenchman named Paul DeJruefé, who had got the film and who asked for two hundred thousand pounds. Before the transaction could be completed, both the British agent and DeJruefé were killed in a Paris bordello.

Colonel von Walter, ex-Gestapo, ex-Madrid Diplomatic Corps, had been working with Boyler since the war. Somehow Von Walter managed to trace the film to José Ruden, in Madrid, whom he knew from Berlin-Madrid wartime associations. Boyler did not know how Ruden came into possession of the film, but speculated that Ruden might have been back of the murders of DeJruefé and the British agent. Von Walter made contact with Ruden and a deal was made, with a big charity bazaar Ruden planned the thirtieth of the month at his Arles villa as the time and place for the transaction to take place.

That is where I came into the picture.

I was to plan and stage a robbery of the bazaar with Von Walter seeing to it that the film was in my possession when I had finished the coup. Boyler had little doubt that the Reds had traced the film to Ruden or that they knew Von Walter was working for the British and he felt sure that anyone making contact with either of them would be suspect. But not I, a criminal with an easily verified background.

Boyler had asked me to state a price for handling the cover aspect of the operation. And I did. To do what he asked, I wanted one hundred thousand American dollars, tax free, an irrevocable import-export permit for Scotch whisky, my Yard file and fingerprint records.

Boyler accepted my price without batting an eyelash. The money and the trade permits would be in my hands the following morning. The Yard file was impossible, being the major factor in the selection for the mission of me, Duncan Reece.

"St. Peter's Square, sir." The driver had stopped near a hotel. I paid him and watched the car disappear into the heavy afternoon traffic. It was exactly five o'clock. I still had thirty minutes to get to the station a half-mile away. I walked around the block, entered the hotel, passed through the lobby to the driveway entrance and caught another cab. "London Road Station."

Two minutes before the train departed, I walked through the barrier and waited until the guard had closed all the doors and the train began to move before I jumped aboard. I was the last one on the train. That was the way I wanted it.

I sat in a Third-Class compartment alone in the dark

and listened to the clicking of the wheels, a little frightened, nervous in the stomach and more aware of danger than I remembered being during the war. Perhaps I was more aware of life? And having enjoyed ten years of peace since the war, I saw how much more there was to lose.

On arrival at Euston Station at nine-fifteen, I cabbed slowly across London, constantly checking my rear for a tag, and found Victoria Station mobbed. It usually is on Friday nights. One way or another the tight travel restrictions have revealed loopholes for the *haut monde* to return to their weekends on the continent. I went directly to my compartment and locked the door, pulled the blinds on the window and sat up until we began to move. I remained upright, listening to every sound outside my door until we were on the ferry.

Fifteen minutes after we had moved out into the channel, I ripped a money belt from my waist and turned on the light. The envelope Boyler had mailed to me through ordinary post was exactly like the first one I had received with preliminary instructions. Plain, white, with no return address.

MR. DUNCAN REECE
care Lion's Head Inn
Rock Ferry, Birkenhead

The paper was tissue thin, neatly typed, double-spaced.

My Dear Duncan:

Until now, you have followed my instructions perfectly. Otherwise you would have been stopped.

Needless to say you have been under surveillance. Your code name is SENTINEL and all contacts to me should be made via air post to March. L. Cassidy, Hotel Bristol, London, S.W. 9, England. A warning here. Do not make this contact unless it is absolutely necessary. There is a gentleman aboard wearing a green scarf, brown Harris tweed hunting jacket and smoking a white S-type pipe. He will, on your advance, supply you with ample money for the mission. Since I contacted you, information has come into my hands that might seriously endanger your life and the successful completion of the mission. While danger to your life is an expected quantity in this line of endeavor, it is of course necessary to aid you as much as possible and thus assure the success of our mutual efforts.

Von Walter was pulled out of the Rhine three days ago. His body showed signs of torture and there was no water in his lungs, indicating he was quite dead before he went in. Whether the Reds knew or now know about Von Walter and Ruden is of course the question. They may have run across Von Walter, simply knowing he was a British agent, and then learned from him about Ruden and the plans. Or they have murdered him before he could mention Ruden.

There is good reason why we don't approach Ruden and bargain directly for the film. We simply do not know where he is. Two weeks of digging has turned up absolutely nothing. We must wait for him to keep the appointment on the thirtieth. The continent is literally crawling with agents from every government on earth after that film. Security has tightened up more than I've seen it since the end of the war. Yet we feel this robbery, that was to be just a cover for Von Walter to slip you the film, can still be turned into a definite advantage. We have kept the Von Walter death a secret, and there is a good chance Ruden does not know he is dead. Therefore he will be expecting Von Walter on the thirtieth, only it will be you—and only you—who shows up, performing a theft of the film along with everything else of value at the villa. We cannot and will not recognize you, or any appeals for help from you once the man in the green scarf gives you the operational money. You are being paid your price for services rendered. Should you be successful and we receive the film, it still does not eliminate you from their reprisals should they suspect you are our man. They must believe, though they do not have the film, that it is unobtainable and in fact has vanished from the face of the earth. Once you get the film, Ruden must be silenced. The film can be identified by the sharp angular printing at the top of each frame—"HOCH GEHEIMNIS" (Top Secret) and the signature "FRITZ HEMER" beneath it.

It must be obvious, Duncan, this is the most important mission of our lives. My insistence on you as the man to handle the job—despite our personal differences—should make that fact obvious.

Good luck,
March. L. Cassidy

I reread the letter four times and then, setting a match to the sheets in the basin, watched them burn to black and brittle carbon before washing it down the drain pipe. I snapped off the light, opened the door and went in search of the man with a green scarf.

2

Cold, bloodless clarity; attack intelligence. A charity ball with international society gambling for the kiddies. That was the way Boyler operated. How many times had we seen the German Corps work out a beautifully balanced plan and then try to force it into the human pattern. Boyler started at the other end, let the human element work out its own abstract designs and acted within them, forcing nothing.

I spent an hour in the diner over coffee, waiting for the green scarf to show up, before deciding to go in search of him. I studied the faces, but did not see any of them. I listened to their eager conversations and heard nothing. I thought about the villa.

Von Walter would have circulated in a crowd like the one that would be at the Ruden bazaar. He had been that kind of a Nazi in Spain. And I, the British criminal, would rob the ball and, in passing, get the film, and should I be caught by the Sûreté I would still be a criminal. If I were caught by the Reds, I would be a dead man.

I finished a third cup of coffee and lingered over a cigarette. For a moment I considered quitting. Return to the Lion's Head and forget the whole thing. But I only thought of it for a moment. It was beyond me now. Much more was expected of me now that L. was a paid mercenary. The patriot might rebel under certain conditions, but not the paid fighter. He was supposed to do a job, get his money and be quiet. Philip Boyler would kill me the moment he suspected he could no longer trust me. A cab would roll out of the fog suddenly—or I would be jostled onto the tracks of a tube station before an express—or there were many other ways. And Boyler? He would regret only that Britain had lost a damn good agent and think nothing at all of Duncan Reece.

I paid my check and listened to the waiter tell me it was the smoothest channel crossing he could remember, gave him a half-crown tip and left.

At the end of the car, at the single-seated table in the corner of the door, a sallow-faced oldish man was eating slowly while reading a newspaper. As I passed him, he turned slightly to the window and scratched his right ear. I could not see his face. I passed on out the door.

There was a party in the second car from mine. The men were all handsome and charming and the women were beautiful and excitingly drunk. I searched their necks for signs of the green scarf. A group spilled out of a compartment, laughing, holding on to each other. One of the youngish looking men had taken a life preserver from the wall and put it over his head. He grabbed a nearby girl and yelled, "Save me, Helen! Save me, I'm drowning!" The others laughed loudly, but it was not very funny. I tried to push past them.

"Well, darling," she said looking up at me. "You look a little old for me, but you're cute. Have a drink?"

"Sorry." I tried to push past her. She wore a brown tweed skirt and a tight-fitting green cashmere sweater. She looked like a playful kitten ready to romp and behave mischievously.

"What's the hurry?" She couldn't have been more than twenty. "It's a long way to Paris, darling." She wrinkled her eyes.

"Yes," I said, trying to squeeze past her. I could make it. The life-preserver comic was about to show how he would dive overboard if the ferry started to sink, and the others pressed back to give him room, still laughing. "I'm busy at the moment," I said to her.

"How can you be busy on a holiday?" She was blonde and pressed up against me. Our thighs touched and then when the comic made his dive, our stomachs were flat against each other.

"It happens," I said, "but I'll take a rain check."

"Well, darling, if that's the way you want it." Her eyes drifted away from my face, interest gone.

The crowd pressed on and I managed to get past her. It was all too gay, too frolicsome. It reminded me of other young faces drawn into hard masks fighting to hide their fear. But they died anyway, with or without their fear showing.

This was the lucky generation, the one that just misses the wars. The age group that lives listening to the sorry tales of the last war and watching the new one loom on the horizon in the daily newspapers.

I found the green scarf in the third car down from mine. He was sitting alone in his compartment reading. I checked him carefully. Everything was in order except the S-type pipe was beside him on the couch. I tapped on the glass and opened the door.

He stood up and stepped forward quickly, his eyes glowering at me. "I say! What do ye want? Here, ye've gotten inta the wr-r-ong compar-rtment, ye know!" He placed both of his palms flat against my chest and roughed up against me, pushing me back out of the door. "Get on with ye! Back to you-r-r dr-r-unken tar-r-ts, eh!" He gave me one last shove, slammed the door in my face and pulled the blind.

I glanced around me. The companionway was empty. At the far end of the car a lavatory door stood ajar. I stepped inside quickly and locked the door. I grinned. Green Scarf knew what he was doing.

I pulled the flat, thick packet from the front of my coat where he had shoved it while pushing me out of the door and stripped the white paper from around five thousand pounds in old bills. On the top bill someone had scrawled in an angular hand: "They board train in Calais."

I stuffed the fifty one-hundred-pound notes into my money belt and buttoned my shirt. I opened the door. Just at that moment the door connecting the cars was opened and I heard the screams and laughter from the party. Life-preserver must be about ready to go out of the window.

I stepped into the companionway and started toward the party car. A man came toward me. He was halfway on me before I recognized him for the sallow-faced man who ate alone and hid his face when I passed him in the dining car.

He weaved slightly with the movement of the ferry. His right hand remained in his jacket pocket while he steadied himself on the railing with his left. His eyes clung to me as we approached each other. I stared at the hand in the pocket, ready to jump.

"Pardon, M'sieu," he said gently and slipped past me, entering the lavatory.

There was a pain in my chest until I realized I had been holding my breath. Drops of perspiration rolled down the backs of my legs.

I did not want to leave the train in Calais for many reasons. Very few people got off there and that would be suspicious. For another, it was important I get to Paris as quickly as possible. It is easier to lose yourself in Paris than Calais.

It was going to be a long night. And I didn't have a gun. I was thinking about how much good it would do for me to lock myself in my compartment when there was a sudden hysterical roar of laughter from the party car. Life-preserver had dove again.

I grinned. That was the kind of party that would last all the way to Paris.

She was backing out of a compartment as I entered. I slipped up behind her and put an arm around her waist. She twisted her body slowly without moving her feet, drunkenly, and fell limp in my arms. "Well, it's you, darling," she said softly, wrinkling the corners of her eyes. She laced her fingers around my neck.

"About that drink—" I said.

"Come along, darling," she smiled, showing small, even white teeth. "Ummmmhm! Yes, you come along with me, darling. You might not be too old for me at that. And you are so very cute."

She took me by the hand and threaded her way down the companionway past the mob to another compartment. "Here is where you get your drink, darling." She closed the door, locked it and turned out the light, climbing into my arms. She made a sound in her throat like a kitten approaching a saucer of milk.

It was a lovely party. A very busy party all the way to Nord Station in Paris. If anyone got on the train in Calais, I didn't know anything about it. And furthermore I didn't care.

3

I spent three days locating Tookie Smith and found him in a Montmartre bistro. He had been drunk for three weeks and I hardly recognized him. After a bath and a shave, a little food and much coffee, he began to look a little as I remembered him—square-faced, thin-lipped, with flaky gray eyes and strong white teeth. He combed his hair straight back without a part and wore it long on the back of his neck.

"Feel better?" I asked.

"No," he grunted sourly. "What do you want, Reece?"

"Have a proposition for you."

"Spill."

"A big coup. There's a charity bazaar going to be held at a big villa near Arles on the thirtieth of this month. I've thought about it a long time. I think it can be had."

"Why come to me?" He looked at me blearily.

"You are the only one I know in Paris able to round up the chaps—the right chaps—we would need for an operation like this."

He nodded gravely. "That's true. I know a lot of people. You got the money to back this kind of play?"

"Enough. I haven't seen the house yet, but regardless of how big it is, it isn't profitable to have more than six men to split. You, myself and four more."

"Must be a big house." He shook his head. "Must be a damn big house. Six men to split." He lit a cigarette, dragged and began to cough heavily. He spit into a dirty handkerchief and looked at it. "How much you think we can make, sweetheart?"

He coughed again before I could answer. Deeply, convulsively.

I said, "My information is that there will be jewels and more jewels, dollars, pounds and francs lying on the tables. This is one of those plush blowouts with picture stars, international bums, lice, louts—you know, the Eden Rock set—loaded."

He nodded appreciatively, got up and began pacing the floor. He dug his little finger into his ear. His short legs snapped forward like they were connected with springs at the hip and knee joints.

"What happened to you after that mess in Cherbourg?" I asked.

"Le Havre. You mean Le Havre," he said. "I lost everything. I had this sailor lined up on a boat to bring the stuff over from the States. Cigarettes, bolts of nylon cloth and some other stuff. Some bastard on the boat caught wise. They met us on the dock. Jesus! There musta been a hundred of them. They let us have it."

"How did you get away?"

"Luck. Just plain stupid, goddamn luck!" he snarled. "I ran off the pier, caught a bus loaded with workers that didn't stop to pick up anyone else, so it didn't stop until it got to the railroad station. I caught the Auto-Rail Rapidé leaving in three minutes. Get that! Three minutes," he held up three fingers, "and in a half hour I was damn near in Rouen. Plain blind luck!"

I asked: "Did you lose much?"

"Every dime," he replied bitterly. "Close to eight grand. But that ain't so bad as the Sûreté knowing I had something to do with it. It ain't been easy to spring a buck since then. Your operation sounds, I say *talks*, like it could amount to something. But I gotta play it mysterious, Reece. They start watching you over here and whammo! you're dead. It's like being a four-time loser back in the States." He stopped his walking and looked at me. "I couldn't get a work permit, and you know what? I been panhandling in the cafés, hitting the GI students for a meal here and there."

"How about your women? Couldn't you get one of them to take care of you?" I asked.

"Sure! For a few weeks. But soon as they don't see no scratch come in, and the Sûreté bouncing me around with questions every time there's a play somewhere in a hundred miles of here, the broads get wise and drop me fast. I even thought about going back to the States," he added a little wistfully.

"Why didn't you?"

"How?" he sneered. "Swim?" He coughed again, harshly, holding on to his stomach. His voice was thin when he came out of it. "I'm Dishonorably Discharged from Uncle Sam's Army. The Frenchies want to send me back—but their consul and my consul been yelling at each other who's going to buy the ticket."

Tookie Smith sat down and swilled another cup of coffee. He stared at his hands in sullen silence. "I'm the best in my battalion, maybe the whole division. Infantry scout. Master Sergeant." He lit another cigarette and puffed nervously. "Sometimes I probe twenty-five miles ahead of everybody else scouting their armor and those eighty-eights. Jesus, what a life. Out there all by myself. Krauts all over the place. All I got to do is shoot with my eyes closed and I knock off a company there's so many krauts. And scared to death. But I liked it. And you think it meant anything I got more decorations than any guy in the division? In a pig's eye! Not when that lousy kraut bastard said I took his diamonds, it didn't. They busted me so fast I thought I was taken out by a Stuka!"

"Did you take the diamonds?"

He sneered at me. "Sure! But that ain't got nothing to do with them believing that kraut-head instead of me. He's down on his hands and knees before the Colonel begging—and I stand there and say, 'Look at the records, sir.' I don't beg. He begs. He gets half the diamonds back. The Colonel gets the other half and I get D. D."

Tookie was a young man. I doubt if he was more than twenty-eight or -nine. He was the man I needed for the operation—a crack shot with pistols, a truly remarkable scout, with nerves that would meet any test. The enemy had gradually changed from the Germans to Army Brass to the Sûreté; and he from a soldier to a common criminal. I doubt if he was aware of it. I think he still imagined himself the bad black sheep of the American Army, whose heroism and decorations entitled him to a certain immunity from authority. Yet this time, on seeing him and listening to his talk, I had the feeling that he was beginning to see the change and was beginning to feel afraid.

I had met him when he acted as contact man for a black market ring I had made a deal with. I liked his manner of thinking and his close touch with the market's needs, and I had made a few private deals with him. The Le Havre misfire was to be the one big coup that would put him in the big time and it had failed.

He looked up at me suddenly. "This has to work, sweetheart. One solid rap on me and that Sûreté takes little Tookie by the hand."

"There's one thing I want you to understand, Tookie. This is my operation, my capital, and I take fifty percent of the coup—half."

He thought that over a moment. "Okay. Fine. You're the boss and you get half. I get the other guys and make my own deal with them, maneuvering the other half any way I want, right?"

"Right." He got up and turned to stare out of the window. "I don't want anyone too experienced in on this, Tookie."

"You mean with a record?" he said over his shoulder.

"I would prefer hungry Frenchmen, if you can find them."

He chuckled. "Everybody in France is hungry."

"Can you get guns?"

"I think so," he nodded thoughtfully. "But they'll cost plenty."

"No matter. I've got money to burn. I expect to make plenty out of this. A hundred thousand pounds."

He turned, his eyes widened. "Your share alone?" He whistled. "That leaves about fifty thousand pounds for Tookie after the others are paid off—that's a hundred and forty G's in the very bright green."

"Can you get Lugers?" I asked. "They're harder to trace."

"There are just as many American forty-fives around. And sweetheart, when you're stuck with a forty-five slug in your gut, you stay down until Jesus comes."

"Forty-fives, then," I agreed, having a healthy regard for the American gun myself. "And I want a car. Can't take a chance on a stolen one. How much for a—say 1950 Dalahaye?"

Rubbing his nose, he said: "That should run into dough. Maybe two, two and a half grand for a good one."

"How much for six guns and plenty of fresh ammo?"

"Another G. The guns and ammo come from NATO GI's. It's all fresh."

I handed over the money. "I want it tonight at the latest."

He grinned and accepted the money "Can't be tonight. Gotta see someone."

I got up slowly and faced him. "Tookie, there's two hundred thousand pounds waiting for us. I spent a lot of time breaking this one down. I say you get the car and the guns tonight—and lay off the women. First woman, and you're out."

He said coldly, "Can't be out. I know too much."

"You can be silenced," I said levelly. "Don't push too hard. This is a break for you—recognize it. Don't throw it away. I'm the boss—got it, Tookie? Got it hard and clear? Nothing is going to stand in my way of this one. I'll stomp you in the ground."

He grinned lopsidedly and shrugged. "Sure. You're the boss. No ladies."

"And you get the car tonight. And the guns."

"Tonight," he said. He moved toward the door. "You know sweetheart, when a wingding like this villa bit gets into the papers, every heist artist in France and elsewhere is going to get the same idea. And that means beaucoup guards at the party." His eyes were flaky and thoughtful. It was the kind of thinking ahead that I had anticipated in Tookie.

"We'll see," I said with a grin. "Incidentally, about the others—what about Marcel Janiér?"

"He wouldn't be interested."

"Why not?"

"Dead."

"Oh! And Jon Luié?"

"Gone to Algiers for six months now. Trying to set up

a weed operation and buck the Italian mobs—but I ain't heard from him in a long time and, bucking the Italians, he could be dead, too." He coughed again and clung to the door frame. When he finished, his face was drawn white. I watched as the blood rushed back into his cheeks. "Try the Diable Rouge and see if Luié is back in town."

"Thanks. I'll try it."

"And, sweetheart, if you take him on, he makes his deal with me."

"With you," I said. "And I want a receipt for the car, Tookie. Nothing hot."

"See you either tonight or tomorrow morning. May take me a while to round up the rods." He closed the door behind him.

I sat down and poured myself a drink. I had my first man and I couldn't ask for a better one. I dressed and shaved and left the hotel for dinner. While it was chilly, I enjoyed the Champs Élysées.

I had walked an hour when I noticed the little man in back of me. I didn't recognize him. I hurried ahead, scrambled across the boulevard and lost myself in the evening rush of the Metro. It was that simple.

<h1 style="text-align:center">4</h1>

Jon Luié was still in Algiers. There was nothing to do but wait for Tookie to return with the car before we could go south. It began to rain on the way back to my hotel and it was a cold rain, making me think of the Lion's Head in Rock Ferry. I settled in bed with a bottle and the evening papers, searching the columns for news of the bazaar at Ruden's. I was struggling through a long paragraph in *L'Aiglon* when there was a knock on the door. "*Entrez!*"

The door opened. "Monsieur Reece?" a voice asked.

He was wearing a soaking trench coat. He pulled his hat off and let it drip at his side. "You are Monsieur Duncan Reece?" he asked.

It was the little man who had followed me early in the evening.

"Who are you?"

"Inspector Roger Delile. Paris Sûreté." He looked down at the puddle of water. "May I come in?"

"What do you want?"

"To ask you a few questions, M'sieu."

"May I see your identification, please?"

He nodded sleepily and walked over to the bed. I could hear water squishing in his shoes. Rummaging inside his coat, he brought out a folded, double celluloid-window case and handed it to me. It could have been a forgery, but I felt it was genuine. I handed it back to him. He yawned in my face and shook his head. He said:

"How long are you going to stay in Paris, M'sieu?"

"I don't know. Why?" I got off the bed and took a cigarette from the night table. I sat down in one of the two chairs and hung a leg across the chair arm. He had not moved, but twisted his body to watch me. He walked to the lavatory door and knocked gently.

"Anyone in there?" he asked.

"Open it and see."

"A woman?"

"Open it and see, M'sieu."

He shrugged and fought another yawn. "What is your business in Paris, M'sieu?"

"Pleasure."

He glanced at the lavatory door. "See that you confine your activities to pleasure. Your papers, please."

I dug them out of my coat pocket and handed them over. He looked at them carefully for a good five minutes. He held the passport up to the light and looked at the watermark, he rubbed the paper between his fingers. He scrutinized my photo and looked at me. He gave them back to me without a word, reached over for one of my cigarettes and lit it. He stared at me through the smoke. His eyes were small and his nose large. It made him look squinty. He sat down on the other chair heavily and stamped his shoes. The water made a sucking sound. He looked up at me and grinned. "Have you got a gun?"

"Gun? Why—no." I resisted an impulse to laugh. "No gun, M'sieu Inspector."

He shrugged again and puffed heavily on the cigarette. "How long will you be in Paris?"

"Two or three weeks. I haven't decided."

"And then you will return to England?"

"Perhaps."

He nodded several times. I thought he was going to break out into solid snoring any moment. He opened and closed his eyes. He got up with a grunt and sloshed to the door. "You will report to the Sûreté every third day, M'sieu."

"Why is that?"

"We do not like having you in Paris without knowing where you are—and what you are doing."

"I wonder why?"

"Possibly it is the companions M'sieu has."

"Tookie?" I said.

"We suspect M'sieu Smith for a number of things."

I said bitterly, "I have a drink with a friend and right

away you suspect me."

"If you do not like it, M'sieu, you can always leave."

"Suppose I find myself unable to contact you?"

"Why would that happen, M'sieu?"

"I could, say, get drunk for three days."

"M'sieur!" He lifted his eyebrows. "I am sorry. Every third day. At noon."

"Am I under surveillance?"

"*Comment?*"

"You were following me on the Champs Élysées tonight."

He looked at me steadily. "We have not been watching you, M'sieu. And please do not fail to report." He put his wet hat on. "*Bon soir*, M'sieu." He closed the door softly.

Why would he say he had not been watching me, when he had? I could have made a mistake about the little man on the Champs Élysées, but I do not make that kind of mistake. He might say he had not been following me to throw me off the track. But the Sûreté does not bait its undesirables.

He would however if he were a Red. And he would be waiting for me to make a move.

I folded the newspapers carefully and turned out the lights. I stepped to the window and looked out. Rue Collord was swept with rain. Nothing moved in the darkness below. I kept my eyes on the street while I slipped on my shoes and waited for perhaps twenty minutes. Then I saw it. A slight movement, something you might not notice in a hundred nights if you were not looking for it, if you had not been trained to wait for it—a furry movement across the street in the doorway of a garage.

I turned to the door quickly, looked outside. The

corridor was empty. Down at the stairwell, I looked over the banister and could see four floors below to the lobby dimly lighted and silent. I turned to the elevator and rang the bell, then ducked back to the stairs and waited until I heard the creak of the lift come to life. Racing down the stairs, I found the lobby empty and turned to the back of the building. A door beyond the desk was open. I went inside and found myself in a pantry. I fought my way through the darkness before I found the back door.

I opened it softly. Behind me the elevator was returning to the street floor. The rain-mist bathed my face. I could see nothing outside but blackness. I had no way of telling if it was a blind exit, but I had to move.

I closed the door behind me and stood still, listening. Nothing but rain. I felt along one wall for a few yards and found another wall, then along that one, around garbage pails, until I came to a door. It was locked. I kept going. At the apex of the third and fourth wall, I found the gate.

Outside the rain drummed heavily on the Belgian cobblestones. I eased through the exit, looked around quickly and moved away from the front of the hotel. At the next corner I broke into a run.

Six blocks later and down as many side streets, I stopped in a deep doorway gasping for breath. Nothing followed. I walked on quickly and at the Rue Santé hailed a cab. "Le Diable Rouge," I said to the driver. I settled in the back, soaking wet.

If Inspector Delile was a genuine cop concerned only with my association with Tookie, there was nothing to be worried about. But if Monsieur le Inspector was not genuine, there was much to worry about. I would have to move as soon as Tookie returned. And Tookie, not finding me at the Hotel Collord, would go to the Diable Rouge.

5

If you've been to Paris, you know places like the Diable Rouge. They are in sections where the elegance has long washed away and they are ugly in the bright harsh light of day. But at night when you go to places like the Diable Rouge, darkness softens the paintless neighborhoods and shadows help to hide the grime.

An American once called a nightclub an upholstered sewer. The Diable Rouge was one of those depressing underground restaurants that serves excellent food and, on the stroke of midnight, closes its kitchen. The lights are dimmed. A four-piece Negro jazz band begins to play, the prices go up a hundred percent and the inferior wines are served. About two in the morning, a nude woman (and in some places it is a nude man) comes out and does a dance bathed in a green light and retires to thunderous applause. Le Diable Rouge is a tourist trap.

I found a table near the door and ordered brandy. I was beginning to dry out a bit when I saw him walk in. He went directly to the bar, sat down with a brandy and began looking around. He was thickset, with blond, close-cropped hair so short it looked bald from where I sat. I had seen too many ex-German soldiers not to know that he was one, even before I noticed the stiff military walk and the peculiar way he held his head. He moved away from the bar toward me, stopped short and dropped me a curt bow. He stood like that waiting for me to look up. When I didn't, he clicked his heels and dropped me another bow. "Monsieur Reece?" he said with a thick accent.

I looked up.

"May I sit down please? I have something I would like to discuss with you."

"Who are you?"

"Otto Lorenz, M'sieu." He clicked his heels and bowed again. "I am a friend of—Tookie Smith."

"That's nice," I said.

"May I sit down?" I waved him to a chair.

"How did you know I was Reece?" I asked evenly.

He smiled smugly. "You have a certain—look about you, M'sieu."

I sipped a brandy and watched a prostitute walk across the dance floor for the third time past a young Latin, who in turn was all eyes for a beautiful young thing sitting with an old man across the room. "What do you want, M'sieu?" I asked.

"Tookie and I are great friends. He told me—ah—certain things about you."

"That was nice of Tookie."

He glared at me, then looked away. "Tookie said you might be in need of men with special talents."

"That was nice of Tookie. He has a way about him."

He got red in the face. His neck became stiff. His hands began to tremble. He put them in his lap. I could see he was fighting for control, and he won it back again. He relaxed. Otto had been well trained.

I said, "Are you in possession of such talents?"

The prostitute came back from the ladies' room and walked past the Latin boy again. She dropped her bag. The boy picked it up. They said a few words and she sat down. The beautiful young thing and the old man were kissing. She could have been his granddaughter. It was repulsive. The Latin saw them and made a face of disgust.

"I believe," Otto said in my ear, "that I might be interested in a certain proposal you might wish to make me, M'sieu."

"I asked you about your special talents," I said, turning to look at him full-face for the first time. "Are you talented, M'sieu?"

He really got stiff then. "I have no papers. Tookie can speak for me."

"How long have you been in Paris?"

"Four years."

"How long have you known Tookie?"

"Four years."

"Wehrmacht?"

He nodded slowly. "Infantry—Eastern Front."

"Nazi?"

He looked at me steadily and nodded his head. "A Nazi, M'sieu. Hitler Youth. I was forced to join."

"Of course," I said lightly.

"Of course?" he said quickly.

I smiled and waved my hand casually. "I meant, M'sieu Lorenz, that most children were taught the comical superman theory in Germany."

That really got him. He had just intimated he was anti-Nazi throughout his enforced membership, and now either had to take what I had said, or defend Nazism. Again I watched him working on that control. It was not easy or pretty to watch. I turned away. "Where did you meet Tookie that he told you about me?"

"Late last evening. In Montmartre. I went to your hotel, but you had gone. Tookie said you might be here."

"What kind of work have you been doing?"

"I would prefer not to talk about it," he said stiffly.

I watched the Latin boy and the prostitute move to the dance floor for a sensual, undulating mambo.

"You would not trust me because I am a German!" Otto hissed in my ear.

"I wouldn't trust you because I don't know anything about you. Tookie likes you, but that's Tookie for you." I laughed. "Being a Nazi German does make it difficult though."

He looked at the table. I could see he was working on that control again. He could get up and stomp out, or slap my face, or he could get control of himself again and take it.

"Black market?" I asked.

He nodded. "With Tookie."

"You in on the Le Havre deal?"

He nodded again. I asked, "How did you get into France?"

"I sneaked across the border. I hoped to find a better opportunity here than in Nuremberg."

"What's that black stuff on your hands?"

He stuffed his hands in his pockets and stared at me sullenly. "That has nothing to do with my talents—or Tookie's reason for sending me to you."

I stood up and threw money on the table. "*Bon soir,* M'sieu," I said indifferently.

I did not expect him to make an appeal to me and he didn't. I threaded my way through the café and out into the chilly night air of the street. The rain had stopped. The red neon sign of the Devil dancing with a nude woman reflected on the wet street.

I was halfway down the block when I heard his quick footsteps in back of me. The corner was just ahead. I quickened my steps and turned the corner, flattening myself against the wall. It was not impossible that he had picked me out of the crowd in the café. Tookie could have given him a good description. But there was one thing gnawing at the bottom of the whole thing. Otto Lorenz was playing too hard to get.

He dashed around the corner, saw me and tried to skid to a stop. I stepped in quickly and hit him in the stomach, and when he doubled over, caught him with a straightened right-hand chop on the neck. He went down on his hands and knees and tried to swing at my groin. I stepped back and kicked him in the face, slamming him back against the wall. I was on top of him before he stopped moving, my thumbs on his Adam's apple. He stared at me, his saucer-blue eyes wide with fright. "Talk!" I demanded.

He made a sound in his throat and I eased up on the thumbs a little. He tried to knee me. I hit him then, five or six times in the stomach. He bent over, fell at my feet and vomited. "Who sent you?"

"Tookie—I swear it!" he managed, and vomited again.

"What did he say?"

"That you were planning a big operation—and needed—men who could take orders and—handle guns."

"Can you take orders?"

He could not answer. I pulled out a wallet from inside his jacket. It contained a letter addressed to Otto Lorenz with Montmartre address, No. 32 Rue De La Cruix, mailed in Nuremberg; an identity card with his photo on it that even in the dark looked forged; a five-hundred franc note, a few obscene photographs and a news clipping about a new law concerning aliens. I slipped them back inside and dropped the wallet beside him. He struggled to his feet and put it away.

"Where were you when Tookie approached you?" I demanded, grabbing him by the arm and twisting it behind him. He didn't answer. I tightened up the arm. "Tookie will tell me—but I want it from you."

He clenched his teeth so hard I could hear them grinding. "*Mein Gott! Ich war ein Schuhwichser in einem Bor dell in Montmartre!*"

"I don't understand German."

"I was—a bootblack—" he stopped and I could feel his body relax—"in a whorehouse. It was the only job I could find."

"And that was where you met Tookie?" I remembered the black stains on his hands. "Was it?" I insisted.

He nodded. I let him go. He fell against the wall, hung his head and cried. "You do not know—what it is like to be a hated enemy—a defeated, hated enemy in Paris—without papers—without money."

I let him cry it out then offered him a cigarette before we headed back for Le Diable Rouge.

We did not talk. He drank several double brandies and massaged his stomach and neck without looking at me once. The Latin and the prostitute had disappeared, but the young thing and the old man were still tight in the corner. He wasn't going to make it, I decided.

It was close to dawn before Tookie arrived, dressed neatly and looking fresh. He was surprised to find Otto. "Did you get the car?"

He grinned and, digging out a receipt, said, "Six hundred thousand French berries for a '51 Dalahaye. I opened her up outside Paris before I took her. She did 127 miles an hour and no strain. I ran a new Caddy into the ground."

"The guns?" I asked, examining the receipt. He had bought it under another name.

"Six nice ones. Got a price for them since I took so many. Guy wanted to know if I was going to start the war over again. Got plenty of fresh ammo—all clipped. It's all inside the spare tire."

"All right. What about Otto?"

Tookie tilted back in his chair and drew heavily on his cigarette and looked at the German coldly. "He's hungry enough to try anything for a living. Take'm or leave'm. You know where I found him?"

"I know. How much did you tell him?"

"That you could use a gunslinger. No more. Ain't that right, Otto?"

Otto nodded his head. He looked at me anxiously. "Okay, Otto. You're in. Tookie is second in command."

"Yes," he said, not able to hide his relief.

"But I'll tell you now, to your face, so there won't be any misunderstanding later. I'm going to watch you, until you prove it unnecessary." He stared at me steadily. "We need a man who is steady with a gun and can take orders. You will take orders or you'll take a slug in the back of the head."

"Is it because I'm German?"

"I answered that for you once. A lot of it has to do with your being a German—a Nazi German. But that's got no place in this show. We're out for money."

His eyes began to glow. "Thank you, M'sieu."

I glanced at Tookie. His eyes held that flinty expression I remembered so well from the war when the cards were on the table and personal death was close around.

"How much will there be in it for me?" Otto asked softly.

"You make your deal with Tookie," I said. "I am financing the whole operation, so I take one-half off the top—down to the split franc."

"I get the other half," said Tookie rocking forward. "You get ten percent of whatever that half comes out to be."

"Will that be very much?" Otto looked disappointed.

"Twenty-five or thirty thousand American dollars. Enough to get you to Argentina with the rest of you dumb kraut-heads," Tookie said with a good-natured grin. "With real papers."

Otto's expression began to change. I could almost see the wheels turning in his head as he figured out my end of the cut. His eyes clouded over. "I don't have any money now—for expenses."

"You won't need it. We're leaving Paris now. Everything ready, Tookie?" I asked.

"Set."

"Let's go," I said.

6

Tookie drove, with Otto beside him. I sat in the back checking and loading the six American forty-fives. The weapons were heavy and powerful and gave you confidence. There was a lot of traffic the first part of the morning, but once we hit the main highways south toward Lyon, we began to have the roads to ourselves. Otto went right to sleep.

"I know two guys in southern France—Marseille. They might be just right for this deal," Tookie said tentatively.

"Who are they?"

"Two wops. Brothers. One of them's from the States. Deported. Used to be a collector and a rackets guy back in New York for a big-league bookie. He lied before an investigation committee and they nailed him on two counts of five to ten for perjury. He put the pressure on his boss to get him outa the can or he'd blow. Uncle Sam shipped him back to his Genoa as an undesirable."

"Sounds interesting," I said.

"Gino Della Vichia. Ever hear of him?"

I had not.

"He's got a kid brother, Marcus, about fifteen years younger'n him that was in the Italian Army. A storybook Fascist that really believed that stuff Fatso Mussy handed out, just like the kraut-head here did in Germany." He indicated Otto. "When big brother Gino came back, they teamed up with a few American-type ideas and started some sort of a racket. Something to do with collections. Numbers, I think. Anyway, they bumped a chiseler and had to beat it out of the country. They been in Marseille ever since."

"How did you meet them?" I asked.

"'Bout the same time I met you. Black market. They took some stuff off my hands now and then. Interested?" He turned around to look at me in the back seat.

"We'll look into it," I said, continuing to clean the forty-five automatics. Once I had decided there was a tail on me, whether through Tookie, or as it could very well be, independently, it was dangerous and foolish to remain in Paris and recruit the other three men, with the chance of being spotted and picked up. Tookie's contacts were just as extensive in southern France as they were in Paris and I felt it better that we get out of the big city as soon as possible.

At Lyon we stopped for a bite to eat and then continued, getting back on the road as quickly as possible. I wanted to make Arles that night if possible. We hit a lonely stretch of road with a lot of trees on either side. Tookie drove with a casual ease and assurance that most Americans possess—one hand on the wheel, arm propped on the door, half turned in the seat talking to me. He was telling me of his misfortunes in the Paris black market when he stopped suddenly and spun around in his seat, staring into the rearview mirror. "I'm going to slow down, boss," he said, "and let that guy pass me."

Training kept me from turning around. "What is it?"

"There's a big wagon been on our tail off and on since Lyon. He won't pass."

He had slowed down considerably. "Is he still there?" I asked. Tookie glanced in the mirror and nodded.

"Step on it. Lose them," I said.

The big car leaped ahead. I pulled to the side of the window and sneaked a look through the rear. It was an Alfa Romeo. It clung to the back of our car, not more than three hundred yards away, as if a line were stretched between us and we were pulling them.

"We're wide open," Tookie said. "I gotta idea to jam them up, wanta try it?"

"Go ahead," I said.

"Hang on. This is something I learned from a flyboy during the war." Otto had not moved from his slumped position beside Tookie.

Tookie gripped the wheel tightly. The car hurtled down the narrow two-laned band of concrete. The dark woods flashed past in a blur. Suddenly he applied the brakes and spun the wheel slightly, moving into the next lane. It happened so quickly, the car behind us swerved to the right onto the shoulder and shot past us. Tookie pulled back into the proper lane with a grin. "Overshooting. They used to do that with the fighter planes when a kraut got on their tail. What do we do now?"

I studied the rear of the car ahead of us. My mind was fuzzy. Who they could be was almost a simple deduction. Who had sent them was the question, and how did they know where we were—and why act so bold?

If this was a Red connecting link between myself and the man in front of my hotel, the possibly phony Sûreté inspector who had followed me on the Champs Élysées, then I had to cut their lines of communication or risk losing the cover aspect of the operation. If there were police in the car ahead of me, I could not afford to be picked up and questioned, and possibly held in jail, for any length of time.

And there was only one way to insure that not happening.

I climbed over to the front seat and handed each of them two of the forty-fives and clips.

"What's this?" Tookie asked surprised.

"Wonder who they could be?" asked Otto softly.

"Cut off at the next road you see," I ordered Tookie.

"That's right up ahead," he said with a queer look at me out of the corner of his eye. "Here we go!" He applied the brakes with his left foot, while holding the accelerator down with his right, the car slowing down under full throttle. He spun the wheel to the right. Trees and shrubbery flashed past as he straightened out, hitting the throttle again.

"Pull over and stop," I ordered when we had penetrated for a thousand yards or so. "Take the keys and hit the trees for cover."

The car ground to a stop, kicking up dust. Tookie was out of the car and into the trees only a second before Otto and myself.

"Here they come!" he said with tense excitement.

The big car pulled up and stopped a few hundred yards down the road. The doors slammed. We could hear them talking. Then silence.

Where had they come from and why were they here? Did they want to kill me? If so, then they must know about Ruden. Or perhaps they did not know, but suspected me and decided it would be better to eliminate me from the stakes altogether and play out their own plans.

Silence.

The side road lay flat and dusty in the hot Lyon sun. Black trees groped about wildly among each other's branches for a little of the hot sun. Where the trees stopped, the fields began, separated by ten- and fifteen-foot hedgerows. Way off I heard the stuttering exhaust of a motor bike trying for the big hill just above where we turned off. More silence.

"If we were hauling cigarettes or nylon, I'd say they were hijackers." Tookie looked at me significantly. "But we aren't, are we?"

"Three of them just moved in opposite us across the road," said Otto.

"Then one is out on the flank," said Tookie immediately. "Now, would he go to his left or right?" He spun around and studied the thick foliage in our rear. "If I was him," he continued, musing aloud, "I would go deep to the right and try to come up behind that hedgerow. Yeah—that's what he'd do." He moved off toward the hedgerow in our rear without another word, snake-bellied to the ground, moving fast, incredibly fast without making a sound.

"Move to the right—a hundred yards behind that big tree, Otto. I'll probe them from the front. You cover me," I said.

He nodded. "Who can they be?"

"I don't know. You wanta go over and ask them?"

He gave me a funny look and moved off. I waited until he was in position and got his nod. From where he was, he could see the whole road. I slipped forward, and had only moved about five feet when they opened up. Slugs tore up the dirt around me. I flattened to the ground and waited for Otto to return the fire. He did. Shooting with precision and care. You could almost time your watch on the interval between shots. Five seconds, eight seconds, fifteen seconds, three seconds and back to five again. Then he would start at the other end; five, three, fifteen, eight and five. The firing across the road stopped. And then sudden rapid fire from behind where Tookie had gone. Someone screamed. Silence again.

I lay flat on the ground, inching back for cover, my nose touching the ground. I passed several anthills and studied the conformation of a wild crocus before I had returned to the safety of a big tree.

A movement behind me caused me to jerk around, bringing up both guns. Tookie, his face eager, was crawling back on his forearms, the two guns in his hands. He slipped down beside me and lay flat on his back. "Look at this."

He threw a breast wallet in my lap. I glanced at Otto. "Keep them busy!"

He nodded and continued firing in his methodical manner. Before I turned to the wallet, I heard a scream from across the road and a thrashing in the brush. We looked up at Otto. He grinned at us and held up one finger.

"That makes two," Tookie said.

"Two?"

"One plus the one who belonged to this," he said, indicating the wallet.

I opened it. There was a half-million francs inside and nothing else. Not another thing. No papers, no cards or pictures. Nothing. Just the money.

"We're rich." Tookie grinned.

"But we don't get a chance to spend it until the other two are out of the way."

"Who are they, boss?" Rolling over to face the road, Tookie spoke to me over his shoulder.

I didn't answer.

"I ask you again, sweetheart," and I felt the barrel of his gun in my stomach, "who are they?"

"I don't know," I said, "and don't be foolish. We've got to get rid of those two across the road."

"I ain't worried about them. I can get those dumb bastards with my eyes closed. I wanta know what this is all about."

"It's a hijack," I said.

"For what?" he sneered. "The car? They got a better car. For your dough? They got plenty." He fingered the francs. "What's up, Duncan?"

The firing across the road started again. Heavy rapid fire directed toward Otto. The German returned it, both hands operating, pacing himself, a sly look on his face—right-hand, left-hand, steady and sure. The firing stopped on both sides for reloads.

Tookie held the gun in my stomach hard and tight. "I wanta answer, boss," he said through his teeth. "I don't mind playing for the big loot and having the odds against you if you figure you can come out a winner. I don't even mind the Sûreté crawling down my neck every time I spit on one of their lousy boulevards, but I wanta know what gives—or I check out now. And I mean now!"

His face was round, sweaty, dirty and tense.

I think I could have killed him. It would have been a fifty-fifty chance, but something stopped me. I stared down at him. Three alternatives. Kill him, lose him or tell him. I did not want to kill him. I did not want to lose him. He was perfect for the operation.

"Last time, boss."

"I'm British Intelligence," I said quietly. "I'm on a mission." I watched him closely.

"Intelligence," he whispered. His eyes opened wide. Comprehension and anger spread over his face. "What is it—a snatch job? A liquidation?"

"Bigger than that, Tookie."

"Bigger," he said thoughtfully. "Germs? The bomb? What's bigger than the bomb?" He lowered the gun.

"I can't tell you that," I said. "But it's bigger."

"Bigger than the bomb," he breathed on it softly. "Jesus H. Christ! You mean somebody figured out something—bigger than the—bomb?"

The air was beginning to grow pungent with the acrid scent of cordite. Otto continued his rhythmic firing.

Tookie stared at me, his face suddenly darkening. "Is this heist job a blind? There ain't going to be no dough?"

"There will be everything I said, Tookie. It's the cover for the operation—but there won't be any operation unless we finish these monkeys off. They've probably been on our tail since I left London. And they wouldn't be here unless they knew what was going on. And from that, you figure one of two things: They were sent to keep tabs on me and have bungled the job, or they were sent along to take care of me. In either case what's to prevent me from cutting their lines of communication back to their proletariat bosses?"

I stopped, looked down at Tookie's frowning face and realized I had been thinking out loud.

"Reds," he breathed heavily. "Listen! I heard you crying after the war was over. They didn't give you such a hot time when Johnny came marching home. How come you're back on the glory road now?"

I said: "For a quarter-million bucks I can pick up at this villa—plus the opportunity to spend it the way I want to."

"Jesus H. Christ!" he snarled angrily. "Ain't enough I gotta beat the law, I gotta get loused up with spy business." He turned to me exasperatedly. "They got Reds crawling outa the goddamn woodwork. You never know when you can trust a guy and when you can't."

Otto yelled at us. "I need more ammo!"

I lifted the gun in my right hand and held it against Tookie's head. "Well, Tookie?" I asked, ignoring Otto.

"Take that outa the back of my head."

"I want an answer."

"I need more ammo," Otto yelled. The firing across the road picked up heavily.

"Take that gun away," Tookie said.

"I'll count three, Tookie. You're in or you're out," I said.

"Okay. I'm in," he growled. "Now take that goddamn gun away from my head or I'll make you use it. Jesus H. Christ! Reds! Fade that one!"

Otto raced over. "What's going on?"

"Shut up kraut!" Tookie said angrily. "You want ammo—you got ammo!" He threw a half-dozen clips at the German's feet. "You take that left hedgerow, I'll take the right. Circle it. Boss, you come in straight through the trees when I give a rebel yell."

"What's a rebel yell?" asked Otto seriously.

"You oughta know, you heard it at Berlin," Tookie said "Gimme five minutes. Okay?"

I nodded.

"Move out, kraut," Tookie said with a grin, his anger fading "We're gonna pincer 'em."

I watched them move off to my left and right. The firing across the road began to pick up as they saw our side moving around. I returned our fire, slowly, trying to pick out movement and gun flashes.

The firing stopped. Voices drifted over to me. Suddenly a blood-curdling scream sliced through the air. It could only have been Tookie making his charge. I jerked up and moved forward with the guns ready, fully clipped. I moved steadily from one tree to another. As I neared the road, they came out of the brush before me firing in back of them. I stood up and fired quickly. They spun around with startled looks on their faces, as if they had both seen the same ghost before their eyes went out, and they fell dead into the dust of the road.

Now there was silence. The eternal stillness that lingers around death.

Tookie crashed out of the trees. He grinned. "Scared the hell outa them with that yell. They musta thought it was an army back there."

"Who *are* they?" Otto demanded, coming up to our side.

"Let's get out of here fast," I said.

"What about the car?" asked Tookie.

I turned to Otto. "Drive it off the road. Tookie, help me drag these two into the trees."

Otto ran down the road and backed the car into the brush. Tookie grabbed the heels of one while I grabbed the others. We pulled them through the dusk back into the brush. Four men. All dead. All dressed alike in black suits. No identification on any of them. One has a wallet with a half-million francs. The car is empty except for cigarettes and clips for their Lugers.

I walked to our car and got in. Tookie drove again. We nosed onto the highway carefully, waiting until there were no cars coming.

I wondered about a lot of things as we sped down the highway. There were a lot of ways they could have sprung to our tail. The Sûreté inspector could have been a phony; or he could have been real and still a Red. He could easily be the reason we were trailed, but again, why so boldly? Was it a lack of technique on their part? And hadn't I run around Paris for three days looking for Tookie? It was not unreasonable to assume the Reds had a dossier on me from the war, and with the panic of the film pressing them, could have spotted me without my knowing it and simply asked for a check on a suspicious and busy Englishman. And that routine check would have revealed my B. I. connections of the war, and the long Yard file since.

Boyler had counted on that, I realized, and had insisted on me personally as the only experienced agent likely to throw them off the track when they sniffed around. The question was: Were they going to be thrown off because I had a long Scotland Yard file?

That was what I thought about while driving down the sunny roads of southern France because I didn't want to think about what I had told Tookie. I couldn't think about it. If I did and started questioning it, I knew I would kill him. And I needed him. And that was one of the crazy, desperate things you do when you've got the world before the muzzle of a gun and your forefinger is on the trigger.

Still, it was hard to accept the fact that they could have trailed me. It would have been damn tough because letting yourself be followed is the kind of kindergarten mistake a good agent never makes. And considering that, the possibility became stronger that one of my boys was a contact for them.

7

I stopped that kind of thinking. I had to start thinking as if there wasn't anything involved but the villa operation. Once inside and the mission was actually being pulled off, then I could begin to think about the film. Until that time, I was a criminal with a bankroll, mapping out a play.

Tookie behaved as if nothing had been said between us. Otto said nothing, but there was thought behind those blue eyes. Thought that went beyond the villa operation. It was not normal for a man to refrain from asking questions after being attacked by four men who wanted to kill you. Both of them were silent, with Tookie's behavior the same as before—chatty and breezy without an apparent care in the world.

In Arles on the Rhone River you can still see the heavy hand of Roman culture, when three-banked galleys ranged the Mediterranean Sea. An arena still stands, and a theatre. And there are many other landmarks to remind you of the city's ancient past. The city spreads itself near the Rhone amid Elysian fields Van Gogh loved to paint. And the gardens are still there. It is a soft country. Nothing moves very fast.

For three days now we had maintained a watch on Ruden's villa. After selling the car in Marseille, Otto had joined us in Arles, coming in alone and establishing himself as an artist. He had brushes, paints, canvas and he toiled in the hot sun nearby where Tookie and I hid on a hilltop settlement of trees. For three days Tookie and I had lived day and night with Otto bringing us food and wine, while he wandered off to make sketches of the villa, its gardens, walls, riverside terrace and the ground around.

Tookie pointed to the three-story pink house in the distance. "I like the idea of there being just one entrance to that garden from this side. You plug that up and cover the river side and nobody moves," he said sucking on a blade of grass.

I looked down at several of the sketches Otto had made of the villa. He could paint well and had a remarkable eye for detail. Beyond the walls of the house, the fields stretched green and hot in the southern French sun. On either side there were magnificent gardens, and straight ahead, below the villa, the Rhone River. A huge grillwork gate that barred the single entrance Tookie referred to had been opened and a man with a donkey cart moved out slowly with a load of clippings from the gardens. They had been working on those gardens all morning. I picked up the binoculars. "Think we can bribe the staff?" I asked. "I'd like to get the layout inside."

"I don't think so," Otto replied. "From what I can pick up in Arles, Ruden's staff has been with him for years. All Spanish and close-mouthed. When the villa is closed, everyone goes back to Spain, perhaps to work in another house." He paused and nodded. "I imagine that is so."

"How many people you think will be here, boss?" Tookie asked.

"Two hundred at least," I replied thoughtfully. "Maybe fifteen or twenty guards, not counting the armed chauffeurs and personal bodyguards."

"Then we're going to need six men," he grunted.

"I agree," said Otto.

"Six should do it," I said, studying the house. "Two men for the front, two for the river side and two on the roof. Where will the cars be parked?"

"How about on this slope?" Tookie gestured to the foot of the hill. "Ain't no place else they can go, with both sides of the house loaded with flowers and stuff— and the fields are too far away."

"That sounds reasonable. And the chauffeurs will assemble on this side of the house around the cars. We take care of them first. Make a note of that Otto—and sketch in a few cars on this slope."

Otto began to sketch.

"There's always a guy with a broad wants to go riding on the river," observed Tookie drily.

"That means guards and attendants," I said. "Two of them at least."

"How you going to take care of them?" Otto asked, gazing down toward the cool waters of the river. "It will be difficult to approach."

I studied the house again through the binoculars. I

ranged up and down the river edges on either side of the villa and came to a stop on a heavy mass of brush and growth a thousand yards away from the villa. I pointed to it. "Two men will hide in that brush several days before the bazaar and move up from there. They take care of the river side of the villa and cover the approach of the roof men, and gain control of the whole back terrace."

Otto made a note of what I said.

"And how do we get on the roof?" asked Tookie. "Fly?" He took a drink of wine and scratched his four-day beard.

"No way to climb up there from the outside," Otto said, examining his sketches and studying the house. "No way that could be depended on."

"The roof men," I explained, "can approach through the gardens, and use a grappling hook and rope ladder for the roof."

They agreed that would probably work out dependably. "What else is there?" I asked.

"How about the guests?" asked Tookie. "We herd them all into one room?"

"Usually the gambling takes place on the second floor. With the ground floor given over to dancing, eating and hoopla," I said. "And the third floor—the bedrooms—used by the guests for their indiscretions."

"Is that what they call it in international society?" grinned Tookie.

"Two men coming down from the hill will take care of the chauffeurs and then move on toward the main gate and take care of the guards inside the walls. River men will cut the main telephone wires—which are to the left of their riverside hiding place," Otto made a note of it, "and converge in time with the front gate men, while roof men strip the upper floors and we meet on the second floor, or wherever the gambling rooms are."

Tookie looked at me. "You still ain't said what we do with the guests."

"Everybody is brought into the house."

"That could prove difficult," Otto said ponderously.

"Not when you shove a forty-five in their gut, it ain't," Tookie said with a grin.

"Get them all together," I said. "That's necessary. You never know which one might be carrying the family fortune, hoping for a big coup—or wearing their grandmother's precious diamond necklace."

"Where do we park our wagon?" asked Tookie.

"It's hidden down the road and we make our initial getaway in one of theirs."

"That's good," Otto said. "I like that."

We were silent a long time, each of us checking over the many possibilities that could ruin the operation and trying to figure out a cover for them. Otto finally spoke. "There will surely be Sûreté men among them. And they will come in police cars—and that means radios. They must be destroyed."

Tookie grunted appreciatively. "Good thinking, kraut."

"Front men will take care of that when they check the cars and cut the distributor cable."

"Jesus!" Tookie exploded beside me. "This is going to be some heist!"

"Make a note," I said to Otto, "to get small scale maps of the entire southern part of France. We've got to get away. It doesn't mean a thing, if we don't get away."

"What about the mountains into Spain?" suggested Tookie. "There must be a zillion cuts through those lousy Pyrenees."

"Get maps of the border check points and the mountains, both sides, Spain and France," I said to Otto. "If we go up, we have to know how to come down."

"If this is one of those crazy party schemes," said Tookie, "you know, where you see pictures in *Life* and *Look*, there will be photographers. Guys with little cameras snapping pictures without your knowing it."

"Pictures can be avoided by wearing masks," I said.

"I don't like masks," said Tookie. "You can't see outa the corner of your eye."

I thought that over. "Then we pull a blackface. Commando style. Everyone in black paint, with black handkerchief over their lower face."

Otto began to sketch Tookie's face, then shaded it black and covered the lower part with a mask. With hats and the black paint, handkerchiefs over our noses and lower jaw, it would be impossible to recognize us unless someone knew us intimately.

"Anything else?" I asked. Neither of them spoke and finally both shook their heads. "All right, let's get out of here. We can always come back for a brief reconnoiter."

Otto picked up his paints and equipment. "You leave before us, Otto. Tookie and I are going to Marseille tonight. We'll take a bus over. Meantime, dig around in the cafés in Arles and see what you can find out about the bazaar. Don't ask any direct questions, just listen."

"I need some money," he said. I gave him twenty thousand francs.

"We'll get another car in Marseille. Stay at the Hôtel de la Posté under the name of Retzien—we'll contact you. If you see us on the street, you don't know us." I lit a cigarette. "All right, Otto, sing it back to me."

Otto repeated the instructions perfectly.

There was an awkward moment when he had gathered up his gear. He didn't know whether to shake hands or not. We shook hands all around. The sun was fading fast as he trudged off toward Arles.

"What now, boss?" Tookie asked after burying evidence of our hilltop observation post of the last three days.

"We skirt Arles and get around to the other side. We wait for the bus. It should be along about nine o'clock—then we go see your friends."

"You'll like these guys, boss."

"We'll see." We started down the back side of the hill.

8

The bus to Marseille was late. Neither Tookie nor I had eaten anything but bread, wine and cheese for three days, and after checking the fourth time with the innkeeper, who made excited and exclamatory calls into Arles, we settled down to eat. Tookie had a coughing fit over an aperitif and had to excuse himself to go to the men's room. He came back ten minutes later, his face flushed red, as I had learned to expect. I did not ask, nor did he ever offer an explanation for his coughing.

We had finished the meat by about eight-thirty and had started on coffee when the door opened and a man more than six feet tall, and with the widest shoulders I had ever seen, entered, looked around, stared hard at us and sat down at a table across the room and continued to glower. He had a heavy neat mane of black hair, harsh dark complexion and flashing even teeth. After ordering wine, he sat smoking a short black cigar, staring at us with hot black eyes and occasionally glancing out of the window.

"Ever see him, boss?" asked Tookie.

"No."

"He's packed."

"He's what?" I asked.

"He's loaded," said Tookie with an impatient wince. "He's got a gun."

"How do you know?" I couldn't see anything.

"Left arm hangs very straight trying to cover the bulge under his arm. Either that or he's got the biggest muscles the world."

"From the size of him, I wouldn't be surprised."

"Wanta brace him?"

"No. He's probably a cattleman. See the way he's dressed?"

"You mean he's a French cowboy?" Tookie asked, screwing up his face. "A French cowboy—well I'll be a sonofabitch!"

I nodded. "Big cattle ranches here on the Rhone Delta. Some of them are as large as your Texas establishments." The big man got up, moving like a ballet-dancing elephant and called the innkeeper. He spoke in French. "When does the bus to Marseille come through?"

"It is late this evening," replied the innkeeper.

The big man grunted and sat back down. He began to shift nervously. He glared at us, but seemed to be more concerned with looking out of the window at the road.

"Let's get out of here," I said to Tookie. I paid the bill and motioned him to follow me. I got up and moved toward the door.

It opened the moment I reached for it. A man in a trench coat and carrying a gun entered, followed by three gendarmes. Tookie started to reach for his gun. I spun quickly, shook my head and nodded toward the big man. Almost immediately the big fellow had moved toward the rear of the inn, the gendarmes and the man in the trench coat after him. Tookie jammed his gun back inside and stood to one side with me to watch.

"Jean Saumur!" yelled the one in civilian clothes. "I order you to stop!" He would be an inspector, I thought.

There was a terrific commotion going on in the back room. The innkeeper began to scream. Dishes crashed to the floor. There were screams and loud socks. And then, like a writhing octopus, a mass of arms, legs and bodies rolled out of the back room. Curses and oaths slashed through the air. Three gendarmes were hanging on to the big fellow who was roaring like an enraged bull. His head was down, shoulders hunched forward, thick arms encircled around two gendarmes, trying desperately to crack their heads together. The other one was on his back, while the inspector pounded him on the head with a blackjack.

The big fellow finally managed to get the two heads together and after cracking them, let go so the gendarmes could roll aside like logs; but the handy work with the blackjack had taken its toll. The big man slumped to his knees, and then everyone started hitting him. He tried to get to his feet and made one last desperate effort to get clear. He swung wildly and caught the inspector in the stomach and sent him clear across the room, sprawling at our feet. Then, I'll swear, he grinned and dropped to the floor out cold. But they did not stop hitting him.

It was over finally. He lay stretched out between the

overturned tables and chairs while the innkeeper and his wife screamed at the unconscious man at our feet. The gendarmes came over and helped him up.

"That," Tookie said, with genuine respect in his voice, "is a hell of a lot of man!"

"Yes," I said. "Quite a bit." It was a little too neat. A little too stagy to be completely believable. Yet no move had been made in our direction. I watched them clamp handcuffs on the giant and lead him past us out of the door.

A grinding of gears and hissing of air brakes brought our attention to the outside. "There's the bus," Tookie said. We left the inn and the confusion, and hurried aboard. A half dozen passengers sat near the front sleepy eyed and stiff, and did not notice us as we made our way to the rear.

Tookie went to sleep at once. I closed my eyes but did not dare to take a chance. I thought about seeing the man enter with the gun. It had happened so suddenly. He could have been after me. He could have killed me. That's the way it will happen, I thought, if it happens.

A half hour later the bus stopped and everyone got off, leaving Tookie and myself alone in the back. We rode bumpily for another hour and a half and I must have dropped off in spite of my caution, because the hiss of the brakes snapped me awake. Tookie stirred at my side. "What is it?"

The door opened. "Marseille, M'sieu?" a voice asked from the darkness of the road.

"*Oui!*" replied the driver.

I nudged Tookie. "Look who's on the way to Marseille."

The big man with the heavy black hair turned to the back of the bus and hesitated a moment on seeing us, then moved on to the back.

"Well, I'll be a sonofabitch," whispered Tookie.

The bus pulled out into the road again. "We could use a man like that, boss," Tookie said in my ear.

I nodded, saying, "But they'll be looking for him."

"It's according to what he's done. And we could keep him under wraps. We wouldn't have to parade him around."

I thought about my first reaction to the appearance of the gendarmes and the inspector at the inn. Had it been too stagy? A little too neat?

Stop it, Reece! How cautious can you get? How impressive does your proof have to be? You'll be jumping at shadows in a moment. "Go feel him out," I said to Tookie.

"Sure, but I'd rather have you there listening to the answers."

"Okay," I said. We moved down the aisle to the seat next to him. "Jean Saumur?" I asked.

"Who wants to know?" He opened one eye. His face was bruised and there were ugly little bumps on his head from the beating he had taken from the blackjack.

"What was the trouble back there in the inn?" I asked.

"Trouble, M'sieu?" he asked in return, shifting his body in the seat and dropping his hand near his shirt front. "I do not understand."

Swiftly and surely, Tookie reached down and jerked the short-nosed gun from inside his shirt. He tried to get up, but Tookie shoved him back into the seat and held the gun on him, covering it with his body from the driver, who was watching us in the rearview mirror.

He glared at us, his hot black eyes flashing in the occasional passing light.

Holding the, gun at the man's neck, Tookie pulled a packet of dirty papers held together with a rubber band from the front shirt pocket. I accepted them and struck a match, turning my back against the inquisitive stare of the driver.

They identified him as Jean Saumur of Avignon. The other papers were nothing but letters, some sort of coupon book and a union card with the grade of journeyman concrete worker. I snapped the band on them and handed them back.

"What is the meaning of this?" he demanded gruffly. "And tell the little one to take the gun away. *Sacré bleu!* I will make him eat it!"

Tookie chuckled softly in the back of his throat. "Take it easy, Frenchie," he said softly. "And keep your voice down."

"What was the trouble back at the inn?" I asked.

"*Comment?*"

"Why did they want you?"

"I hit a man—when he threatened me, like this little one here with the gun," he said in a low, tense whisper. "Phuff! I broke his face."

"What's with the gun?" asked Tookie. "And keep it soft."

"I always carry a gun," he said in a whisper.

"Why?" I asked.

"*Sacré bleu!* You ask a lot of questions, M'sieu!" he said.

"The Sûreté will ask more than that," Tookie said.

"Why were you going to Marseille?" I asked.

"More questions," he replied.

"We have a proposition," I said to him, with a glance at Tookie. The driver was no longer paying any attention to us.

"What kind of a proposition?" he asked carefully. Tookie looked at me. It was my decision to make. I took a deep breath and reminded myself I was thinking like a criminal now, not an intelligence agent. I had a robbery to think of. A big villa. I needed men, and counting myself, Tookie, Otto and possibly the two Italians in Marseille, the big giant would make six.

I asked, "Do you know the Arles section?"

"*Oui*. I was born and raised in Avignon, M'sieu."

"Do you know the Ruden villa in Arles—on the Rhone?"

"*Oui*." He looked at me and then at Tookie suspiciously.

"There's going to be a charity bazaar at the Ruden villa on the thirtieth of this month. We, along with others, plan to do a little gambling of our own that night."

"*Sacré bleu!*" He stared at us. He was genuinely surprised.

"Are you interested?" I asked.

His dark brow creased. "How much is there to be had?" He rubbed his fingers together.

"I am financing the whole operation—and I take half of whatever there is," I said. "Tookie gets the other half—"

"Tookie? That is your name, Tookie?" He twisted around.

"Yeah."

"It is a funny name."

"Yeah. Laugh it up, Frenchie," Tookie said.

"You make your deal with him," I said. "If you want in—okay. If you don't—" I shrugged.

"And if I do not, M'sieu?" he asked softly. "If Saumur does not?"

"Don't talk about it, Frenchie," Tookie said. "You're in or you're out."

"How much?" he asked in a flat hard tone that was still soft.

"Ten percent of my half," Tookie said.

"Of how much?"

"We figure to do a rough half million—"

"Francs?" asked Saumur.

"Dollars, Frenchie. Five hundred thousand kickers from Fort Knox in Uncle Sam land. You get ten percent of half—which should be about twenty-five or thirty grand."

"M'sieu—you are certainly joking," he growled.

"We do not joke," I said. "Are you in or out?"

"Most certainly, M'sieu, I am in! *Sacré bleu!*"

"Good. Tell him, Tookie," I said.

"This is the boss," Tookie said, returning Saumur his gun. "And I am the second boss. You take his orders."

"I take his orders," Saumur said flatly. There was no nonsense in that voice. "For thirty thousand dollars, I will take his orders."

That seemed to settle it. I turned back to my seat, but stopped and turned back to him. "How did you get away from them? They had you handcuffed—and there were four of them."

"M'sieu," he began apologetically, "I am a big man, a cattleman, M'sieu. I am used to space around me. Space to drink, love, fight. I needed space to fight those pigs. Ahhh," he said deep in his throat, "You should have seen them flying. You would not believe how strong I am, M'sieu."

Tookie looked at me and shrugged. "I believe it," I said.

9

It was 2:00 A.M. before the bus pulled up to a stop before a foul-smelling depot off the Canebiére. Marseille was quiet. The filthy, ancient, cynical black hole of the Mediterranean Sea was asleep. Only on the Boulevard Canebiére does Marseille rival Paris in the tradition of magnificent boulevards and avenues. And at night when the lights are on, it is one of the most glorious thoroughfares in the world.

We found a cab on Boulevard Garibaldi, and just to make sure there was nothing in back of us, I doubled back and forth several times, finally returning to Garibaldi for another cab. Tookie gave the driver an address in the port section of the city. "They run a happy house for sailors. It's in back of the café. But Gino and Marcus ain't exactly pimps. They just operate this joint, more like managers, for a big syndicate. It's the biggest outfit on the continent," he went on, explaining, "Gino gets fifteen percent of the take from the house. They do maybe two, three bills a week to split between them."

"Not much."

"They rotate the girls every two weeks—get 'em from Italy and the West Zone mostly."

"Transporting them across borders? United Nations would be interested in that," I said.

"What transport?" Tookie said indignantly. "I said it was a big outfit, and it is! They come across in chartered planes. The girls work nine months a year and then can quit if they want to. Half of their dough goes into the bank in Switzerland for when they've finished their tour—and they get protection. That's the only way they can get the high-class type dames they do. No monkey business. It's strictly international trade—sometimes a dame goes two or three tours—and retires to South America with respectability and a bankroll."

Saumur grunted. But I did not know whether it was in disgust or appreciation for the streamlined management Tookie described.

We left the main streets of the city and were entering the port section. The streets were dark and the blank brick walls of the monotonous rows of warehouses on either side echoed to the stuttering exhaust of the cab ominously. We rounded a corner and ahead was the weak light of an all-night café. In the distance I could see the outlines of the ships riding anchor on mooring buoys, waiting to get alongside the piers inside the sea wall. There was no moon and it was very dark.

Tookie paid the driver and motioned us to follow him inside. The café was a dungeon of dirty whitewashed walls, a galvanized iron bar, wire tables and chairs. There were no women and every chair was filled.

The bartender looked up from pouring a glass of wine and gave us a flat, level appraisal. He was a rough looking man with remote eyes and deliberate movements. His voice, when he spoke to Tookie, was tired and uninterested. *"Bon Soir*, Tookie."

"Hello, Pipi," Tookie said, and waved us to stay behind while he disappeared through a back door. The bartender leaned his fleshy arms on the dirty iron bar and seemingly forgot we were there as he explored his right ear with a dirty finger. A few minutes later the back door opened and a short dark man near fifty, with a heavy, recently-shaved black beard walked toward us; Tookie was behind him.

"Boss, this is Gino—Gino, the boss," Tookie said and moved to one side.

"Boss what?" asked Gino, looking me up and down.

"The boss," Tookie said, putting emphasis on the two words, separating them so they were not related.

Gino nodded. "How do you do?" he said in a voice which was deep and controlled. He spoke with an American accent that was softer, lighter than Tookie's. Gino Della Vichia was several inches under six feet, broad through the chest, with sloping shoulders. His features were composed into a passive expression that would not change often. We shook hands.

"Gino," I said, nodding.

"It is much nicer inside," he said and invited us past him with a nod of his head. We followed through the back door, Saumur lumbering slightly in the rear.

We passed through a long hallway with rooms off to one side, and then into the main sitting room. It was tastefully furnished in maroon and gray. Four or five couples, all of them well-dressed, sat about on the maroon and gray furnishings, drinking and talking in soft secret tones. Gino led us through the room, smiling and speaking to several of the men and girls, into a kitchen. He closed the door. The kitchen was gleaming white, immaculate, with an eight-burner electric stove along one wall, an American washing machine and dryer, and at the far end, an ironer. A huge restaurant-sized refrigerator covered most of the other wall. A porcelain table was in the middle. Tookie walked directly to the refrigerator, opened it and began rummaging around. Saumur joined him. They settled back with a hunk of cheese and bottles of wine. "Nice setup, eh boss?"

"Very nice."

Gino sat down at the table and folded his hands. "What is your name, sir?" he asked politely.

"Duncan Reece."

He nodded and smiled. "What's on your mind, Mister Reece?"

"Tookie said there were two of you," I said. "And call me Duncan."

"My brother Marcus. He'll be along in a minute. Would you like something to eat?"

"Nothing, thank you."

He nodded, got up and walked to the door, saying something to someone beyond. He spoke in Italian. "He should be here in a minute," he said, sitting back down. He pulled out a pair of horn-rimmed glasses and adjusted them carefully, before spreading a French newspaper before him on the table. He glanced up suddenly. "Pardon me. I am interested in horses. Are you a horse player?" he asked softly.

I shrugged. "Only incidentally."

He smiled slightly and turned his attention to the paper. Saumur and Tookie exchanged looks with me and continued to eat.

Ten minutes later, Gino got up, put the glasses away carefully and smiled at me again. He went to the door. This time he spoke in French. "Get that bastard down here! Tell him he can go back to her in an hour. This is business."

He turned to me, and in the manner of a bewildered, tolerant father, explained softly. "My brother likes one of the girls just in from Italy. She has gray eyes and black hair. She fascinates him." He spoke as if it were all a mystery to him.

"How's business, Gino?" asked Tookie.

"This business is always good," he said gently.

The door opened and a young man about twenty-eight or -nine stepped inside. He was tall and thin, too thin, with delicate bones. He leaned against the door and held the knob behind him. A small gold ring hung in the right lobe of his ear. He was barefoot and wore a white silk pullover shirt, stuffed a little too casually into the top of gray flannel trousers. He arched his slim neck to one side and looked at me, hot black eyes insolent; then flicked his gaze over to Tookie and Saumur.

"My brother Marcus," Gino said. Brother Marcus nodded. Gino turned to me, folded his hands on the table and waited.

I told them of the villa and the prospects, everything except the real reason.

"And how much do you think will be there?"

"I figure it should run at least a half-million dollars," I said. "But whatever it is, I take half."

Marcus threw back his head and laughed. "Half!" It was a little too forced; a little too much the actor.

Gino showed nothing. "That's a lot. Fifty percent of a half-million." He shook his head slightly.

"Those are the conditions. I'm backing the whole show. My capital. I take half the gross," I said.

"How many are there to split the remaining half?"

"Five. But that's left up to Tookie," I said.

"Tookie?" Gino was surprised. "Why Tookie?"

"He's my lieutenant," I said.

"Your *lieutenant*," drawled Marcus sarcastically. His French was thick with Italian vowels. He pushed away from the door and walked softly toward me. He stood very close to me, leaned one hand on the table top, the other on his hip. His sleeve fell back revealing a thick, gold identification bracelet. "And what are we supposed to be? Sergeants? Or perhaps privates, eh?" He cursed in Italian and walked away to lean on the refrigerator.

I had stated my price and conditions. I turned to Tookie. "I thought these two were experienced and on the lookout for something."

Tookie rocked forward in his chair and put his hands flat on the table, "You make your deal with me, Gino, if you want in."

"What does that mean?" Gino asked, turning sideways in his chair, one arm resting on the table, the other propped on the chair back, smoothing his hair.

"Say there's a half-million in rough figures. Half goes to the boss here. I take the other half and make a price with you. I already have two others in for a percentage."

"Six men! For a job like this? What are you afraid of?" Marcus said loudly.

"Shut up," Gino said.

Marcus started for the door. "Throw them out, Gino."

Gino looked and spoke to his brother tiredly. "How long do you think I'm going to sit here and play towel-boy for a few yards a week? I get sick every time I think about playing stooge while other guys play games." He turned back to me. Marcus leaned against the door again. "What do we do?" he asked me.

"Whatever I tell you to."

He closed his eyes, then opened them slowly. "What does that mean?"

"I know what I'm doing," I said.

"You want gunmen, protection, is that it?" he asked thoughtfully.

"More or less," I said.

He thought a moment, turned to Tookie and said, "Half of what you get, Tookie. That's twenty-five percent of the whole. It figures to be one-two-five grand on a rough half-million."

Tookie smiled. "Come again."

Gino opened his palms and lay them flat on the table. "That's it, Tookie. I'm no punk. I know how to operate. I've been in on some big heists back in the States."

"Come again," Tookie said.

Gino smiled and pulled his shoulders back. "Make me an offer."

"There are two guys already in," Tookie said. "Saumur here, and a German GI. You know the kraut. Otto Lorenz. He hustled shoes in that joint you used to have back in Paris."

"Otto, eh?" Gino smiled. "I know Otto. Good man."

Marcus laughed again. He lunged away from the door, spread his legs, and stuck out his well-shaped jaw. "Otto," he whispered, "Otto—the shoeshine boy!" He laughed again.

Gino slammed his fist down onto the table and spun around. "Shut up, you goddamned bum!" Marcus darkened visibly and stood still. They glared at each other. Gino turned back to Tookie. "What are you paying the others?"

"That's none of your business," Tookie said.

"Make me an offer," Gino said again.

"Can you control him?" I asked, nodding toward Marcus.

Gino looked at me impassively. "He's my brother. We go together. Make me an offer, Tookie."

"I know he's your brother," I said. "I asked you a goddamn question. Can you control him?"

"If I think he needs control." Gino looked at me with the dead, lidless eyes of a snake.

"Sixteen percent for the two of you," Tookie said.

"Not enough." Gino turned to me. "I've got two

Thompson submachine guns and plenty of ammo. That oughta be worth something."

"I'm supplying the guns. I'm supplying everything."

"Cars? I can get you good cars. Hot, but they're done over so they can't be traced."

"We have everything, Gino," I said, "but two more gun hands."

"Twenty-two percent," said the Italian to Tookie.

"Sixteen," replied Tookie, making a small sound between his teeth. We were silent. The refrigerator kicked over and began to hum. Saumur lit a cigarette. Gino poured himself a glass of wine from Tookie's bottle and sipped it carefully. He sat sideways again and smoothed his hair. He said, "You're backing this thing, eh?"

"Right."

"Make me an offer. Now. In cash. We go with you, help pull the job and take care of ourselves afterwards. We'll go—for fifty grand in cash—half now, half afterwards. Say thirty days after, so you can cool your heels."

"You make your deal with Tookie."

"I'll give you eighteen percent, Gino," Tookie said carefully. "And you throw in the two Thompsons."

"Twenty. We gotta have twenty—ten apiece."

"You're worth ten," Tookie said levelly, "but he ain't."

He looked at Marcus. "He ain't worth five—he ain't worth nothing."

"You say that to me!" Marcus hand flashed inside his shirt at the waist.

He came out with a short-nosed, thirty-two belly gun. Saumur must have moved along with him. No sooner was the gun out, than a bottle of wine flashed across the room and caught Marcus on the shoulder.

Gino was out of his chair and onto Marcus instantly, slapping his brother across the face, speaking heatedly and rapidly in Italian. Marcus looked at me and then toward Tookie, who had his forty-five out and ready. Saumur lounged to one side.

Gino turned back toward me and dropped Marcus' gun on the table. "It won't happen again. I give you my word."

"Your word?" I said gently.

"You can put Gino Della Vichia's word in the Chase Bank and make book on it." He turned back to Tookie, all business now. "We got to have ten apiece, Tookie. That's around fifty grand. We can do something with that kind of heavy dough. I'm worth it to your play, Reece."

"Eighteen," Tookie said. "And that's it."

"Give him twenty," I said, staring at Gino.

"Now wait a minute, boss," Tookie said, swinging around to face me. "I know guys that will spring for a lot less."

"Yeah."

"Boss, you said—"

"Give them twenty," I said.

Tookie's eyes flaked over. He grinned. "Okay," he said. I think he understood. Gino was a good man. It was another plus sign for my mission. Tookie was playing it blind with me. I knew it. He knew it. It was an agreement that needed no words.

"Okay, Gino. Twenty percent of half. That's ten percent of the whole, right?" Tookie said.

"Right."

"You got it straight, Gino?" I said. "I'm holding you responsible for Marcus—no more juvenile behavior. And both of you understand this—I'm the boss."

Gino looked at me impassively. "All right, you're the boss."

"When can you leave here?" I asked, nodding toward the room outside where we had heard laughter and giggling.

"Two days. Until the syndicate gets another man down here."

"Tookie told me of your record back in the States and in Italy. Are you clean in France?"

"Could I operate here if I wasn't?"

I said, "You could, if the syndicate wanted you to."

"You're a pretty smart man," he grunted, with a small smile. "I'm clean, so's Marcus."

"Have you got any money?"

"What kind?"

"Operational," I said. "Here, I'll give you—two hundred thousand francs for expenses—that comes off the top when we cash in. All expenses are deductible—then we split the net."

He nodded and smiled again. "I used to know a cashier for heist mobs in the Midwest. Guys would map a caper and he would invest—for a percentage of the take. He kept books and actually made out his income tax report, listing the car, guns, ammo, everything as a business expense. Got away with it, too. They knew just how much was taken on each job, see, and what the going percentages were for a banker like him. They left him alone, too. Of course," he sighed, "they caught him eventually."

"I'll be in touch with you. And get your hands on the Thompsons."

He nodded and accepted the money. He counted it right there in front of me. He was a very methodical man. I liked that, to a degree. Methodical men have a way of falling apart when the method fails.

We said good night and shook hands all around. Marcus did not shake hands.

I had my crew. I had my assignment.

We all checked into different hotels. We would meet the next morning and go over a list of things we would need during the preparations, and buy them in Marseille.

After a shower and shave, I called for room service and ordered a bottle of brandy, soda and ice, Camembert cheese and brown bread, and an air mail stamp. I listened to Marseille rumble on through the night from six floors above Avenue Caliûre and thought about five professional criminals who behaved like businessmen.

Now that I had them, I had to check them out.

The boy brought the tray and dug the stamp out of his pocket, looking at me sleepily and wondering just a bit if all Englishmen were not completely mad. He did not even brighten when I gave him a five-thousand franc note, and he left me yawning.

I mixed a drink, broke bread and bit into the cheese. I wrote out the names of the five men I had gathered around me on Hôtel de Uhlée stationery, giving background, as much as I knew it, and full descriptions. I stamped the envelope and addressed it to March. L. Cassidy, Hotel Bristol, London, S.W. 9, England. I sat there holding the letter in my hands, thinking, then opened it and added the name of Inspector Roger Delile of the Paris Sûreté. At the bottom of the sheet, I lettered—Re: Marseille Drop, 1941, and the single letter S.

I had another drink and carrying the glass in my hand, walked down the hall to the letter drop beside the elevators and mailed it.

I locked the door to my room, studied it carefully and walked to the window. There was a ledge four floors below me and another two floors above me. I locked the window. I pulled a chest of drawers, with a heavy mirror wobbling crazily, against the door and put a chair on top of the chest. If anyone came in, they would have to break the window or push the chest, making the chair fall.

I piled the pillows in the bed like a body, turned out the lights and crawled underneath, fully clothed, the forty-fives in my hands.

It was cold and hard, but I was too tired to care.

10

In 1941 I had dropped into France and worked out of a bookshop in Marseille for nearly four months without once leaving the back of the shop. It had been one of Boyler's most successful depots for getting agents in and out of France and for RAF pilots shot down.

As soon as the day broke, harsh and bright, I realized I had made a mistake that might be disastrous. I had told Boyler to answer me, using the old drop as an address, without making sure it was still there.

I checked the windows and pulled the chest of drawers back. I was supposed to meet Tookie and Saumur at eleven. It was just past nine as I slipped through the lobby unnoticed.

On the Canebiére I caught a cab and rode up and down looking into side streets until I found one that looked familiar, got out and walked toward the block where the bookshop should be. I walked past it and looked in.

I breathed a sigh of relief. The stalls and the counters were just as I remembered them. It would not be open for another hour, 10:00 A.M., a sign said hanging in the door. I found a café several blocks away and read the morning papers over coffee and bread.

There was still no mention of the four dead men in the Lyon woods. For France, which loves a good murder mystery as well as New York or London, I thought that was significant. Like finding dirty fingermarks on the cookie jar.

I walked back to the bookshop at five after ten. The dust covers were still on the tables. A little man in slippers came out of the back, glanced in my direction and adjusted his glasses.

"Monsieur wishes?" he asked in a thin voice I remembered.

"An Alphonse Lemerre edition of *Le Rouge et le Noir*," I said casually.

"*Mon Dieu!*" he whispered, and took a step toward me, his face lightening up. "M'sieu!"

"Hello, M'sieu Hugh," I said gently.

He reached for my hand and gripped it tightly. "You—you!"

"How are you?"

"*Mon ami*—how are you? What are you doing in Marseille?"

"I cannot tell you. This is not a visit—business."

"Business?" his eyes clouded. "You mean you want to use my store again?"

"Just for one letter," I said gently. "I'm sorry I cannot stay and talk with you—" I shrugged. "It has been a long time, hasn't it, M'sieu? We won, didn't we?"

"*Oui*," his eyes filled up. "We won!" He gripped my

hand. "It is so good to see you again. Tell me one thing before you leave; that young boy who was with you on that last drop—when was it?"

"In 1941—December, '41. It was cold."

"What happened to him? Did he get through safely?"

I shook my head.

He released my hand and turned away. "That one! That *one!* He sat back there reading—reading—"

"A letter will come. Hold it for me." I pressed several hundred thousand francs into his hand and turned toward the door.

"What is it now, Duncan?" he asked standing still, staring after me. "Who is it this time?"

"I cannot tell you that, M'sieu Hugh."

I smiled and walked out of the door, glanced around and hurried toward the boulevard, and down it several blocks before hailing another cab. For six years we had played tag under the noses of the Gestapo with Hugh Roil as the most important drop in southern France. Boyler would have to check the files, but he would find out where to send the answers to my letter.

Tookie and Saumur were waiting for me at eleven. Both of them had bought new clothes. "What now, boss?" Tookie asked me.

"Saumur is going to buy enough food and wine for six men—for a week at least. Basic stuff, Saumur," I said. "Cheese, brown bread, tins of meat." I gave him money. "You understand?"

"What shall I do with it after I buy it?" he asked.

"Have it packed in cartons and take it to your hotel. We'll contact you."

He nodded. "When will that be?"

"When I get ready. Hang around your room."

"*Oui,*" he said, then turned and walked away.

"What's the idea, boss?" Tookie asked.

"You'll see. I want you to buy another car. Make it a different make from the Delahaye. Meet me here at six o'clock this evening." I counted out money and handed it over to him. "That enough?"

"Plenty."

"Six this evening," I said.

He nodded and turned away. He caught a cab at the corner and moved into traffic.

I hurried to the corner and climbed into the back of the next cab in line. "Sûreté," I said in my best French. "Follow that gray cab ahead—see it?"

"*Oui*." The driver dropped into gear and we shot after Tookie's cab.

"Careful," I cautioned. "Not too close."

"*Oui*, M'sieu Inspector."

I trailed Tookie from one motor pool to another. I watched him get out and look over the cars, speak to the salesmen and deliberate carefully. At the fifth stop, Tookie did not go into the shop itself. He went directly to a bistro halfway down the block. I got out of my cab and paid the driver. "*Merci*," he said, surprised.

I waited until he had pulled away, keeping my eyes on Tookie, and then walked slowly after him. I walked past the bistro and glanced in. I did not see him. I came back and stepped inside. I held on tightly to both forty-fives deep in my pocket.

Tookie was not in sight. I walked to the bar. "Cognac," I said.

The woman behind the bar nodded. I watched the door to the rear. "What's back there?" I asked when she poured the cognac.

"Why, M'sieu?"

"Why would a man go back there?"

"Why, indeed?" she asked, her eyes fading into no expression at all. "What does M'sieu want?"

I was about to speak when the door opened and Tookie stepped through. He saw me immediately. His eyes flaked over, his face suddenly setting hard, and then broke into a grin. Tookie knew. He understood perfectly. He walked over toward me, his eyes on my pockets. "Don't jump, boss. Just ask her and the old man all the questions," he said to me in English. He put both hands palms down on the bar.

"Who is this man?" I asked her.

"A friend."

"What kind of a friend?" I asked, as the door opened again and a little man stepped through. He did not appear to notice us and walked behind the bar. He spoke to the woman as he opened a little book and began making notes. "A *very* large bet."

"Ask him, M'sieu," the woman said to me.

The old man turned, and on seeing Tookie, smiled.

"You changed your mind, M'sieu Tookie?"

Tookie shook his head.

"You need a cognac, maybe? That was a pretty big bet, *mon ami!* Perhaps you will need a drink when the horse loses, eh? But it is too late," he said brusquely, "you have already made the bet."

Tookie looked at me. "Okay, boss?"

"What horse?" I asked.

"Sea Queen," said the old man. "Why do you ask? You want to make a bet, M'sieu?"

"What track—what race?" I asked. Tookie did not move.

"San Riatá—Madrid," the old man said slowly, looking from Tookie to me. "The first race," he said softly, sensing something was wrong. "Yes, it is the first race."

I asked, "What's the price?"

"Eight to five, M'sieu," he said. "Was it stolen money?" he pleaded with Tookie. Tookie did not move a muscle. I walked over to a table and picked up the paper. I thumbed through it quickly and found the charts. Sea Queen was running in the first race at San Riatá—probable odds, eight to five. I walked back to Tookie. "Where's your chit?"

He put his hands in his pockets slowly. I stepped back a few feet, watching him, gripping the two guns. I felt the sweat running down my back. He smiled and pulled out the slip of paper. I read it. He had bet one hundred thousand francs to win.

"*Why?*" I felt myself go inside. I pulled my hands out and fought the clenched fingers into relaxing.

"It's a boat job. Gino told me about it last night—"

I drank a cognac quickly. You came close, Tookie, I thought; I'd kill you now, but I need you. But you had time to leak it, Tookie, you had plenty of time. I should kill you—

"What's the matter with you, boss?" Tookie asked at my side. "You look like you've seen a ghost!"

"Yeah. Just tired. Come on, let's get out of here."

We moved back out into the street. I watched him walk ahead of me as we searched for a cab. You had time, Tookie, I thought, and there was someone outside my hotel window, and that Sûreté inspector was right on the spot and lied about following me on the Champs Élysées. And who was it on the road outside of Lyon? Maybe you don't know, Tookie. Then again, maybe you do ...

"Here's the cab, boss." Tookie stood with the door of a cab open, waiting for me to get in. I had not even seen it stop.

We headed down the boulevard, with Tookie giving the address of an auto garage. He settled back. "I'm glad you're a cautious guy, boss," he said. "I really am. You might not have gone to the trouble of finding out about the horse. And it really is a boat job. Gino can check it out for you."

I was silent. "But I can't figure it for you, boss," he continued solemnly. "You come pick me up and give me a rumble about a heist job and then I discover I'm in a tank with live lice who are trying to get me and it's so big I don't know what's going on, and I ain't going to find out. And I don't get nothing for it, so I don't think about it. I'm in on a wingding for loot—but don't brace me every time you get the jumps or you might find trouble. You got your problems—I got mine. Keep yours to yourself—and I keep my own nose clean."

It was a long speech, delivered in deliberate slowness and without emphasis.

"You bought me for a price—and you get what you paid for," he said finally. "No more, no less."

"Let's get the car and pick up Saumur," I said.

I shook my head. I had to stop this. You almost killed him for nothing because, like he said, you're jumpy and afraid and shouldn't be here at all. Boyler made a mistake. You're not the best agent for the job. Your nerves are gone, Reece. You've had it.

But I couldn't pack up and go home to tea.

At the fourth garage-auto pool, Tookie bought a 1952 Mercedes four-door. It was a good car, better than the Dalahaye and newer. We spent the rest of the day making a deal with a fence for six walkie-talkie sets he had bought from GI's in NATO, and a huge battery receiver powerful enough to pick up BBC, RADIO PRAGUE, ROME and MADRID. The lot cost us nearly a half-million francs, but as Tookie said, it was one more plus sign toward success. If success was going to be had.

We found Saumur in his hotel room amid a dozen cartons. Enough food to last a full squad of men a month. "I eat a lot, boss," he said by way of explanation, a wide grin on his rugged face.

After we had loaded the food into the car, leaving half the wine in the room, I stood on the sidewalk and watched the shadows creep up on the streets as the sun dropped. "Here's where we part company," I said. "Saumur, you take the car and go to Montpellier. Stay at the Allier Hôtel until I get in touch with you."

"*Oui*. What about the food?"

"Leave it in the car," I said. "And while you're there, buy new tires all around. Get them at different places. Go down to Narbonne and over to Bésiers and even to Carcassonne."

"*Oui*. I shall use the name of—" he thought a moment—"Jean Coté."

"Jean Coté," I repeated and nodded. He drove off into the traffic with a wave of his hand.

"What about me, boss?" Tookie asked.

"You leave now, by bus for Arles. Check into the Hôtel de la Posté under the name of Kent—unless they demand your papers, then use your own name."

"Anything else?" he asked.

"Just get into the cafés and see what you can pick up in the way of information about the Ruden bazaar. Don't try to get too close. They'll be expecting something. And besides, we have Otto already established."

"Check. When will you be in?"

"I'll follow you in a day or two by bus. And the Italians should be along by the end of the week."

"What was the food for?" he asked suddenly.

"To eat," I said. "We're going to make like commando troops and practice dry runs."

"You're kidding!" he said.

"You'll see."

"Take it easy," he said. "I'd hate to pull this off without you."

"I'll be around," I said.

I watched him walk off down the Canebiére, his short legs snapping out in front of him quickly. I thought about his moving through the brush in the hot sun in the Lyon woods, taking care of the mysterious four— how easily he had taken care of the man trying to flank us. How contemptuous he was of them and their guns when he had decided it was time to finish them.

I sat down at the nearest table of the nearest café and ordered cognac. I was suddenly very tired and depressed. The thing was rolling now. Nothing would stop it. I felt that. Sitting there in the thickening shadows and the electric lights coming on, I watched the cars swoosh past on the boulevard.

I had another drink and ordered cheese and bread. I can't ever remember having cheese, bread and cognac taste so good.

11

The depression remained with me all night and all the next day as I hung around the public gardens waiting for Boyler's answer to my letter. A new conviction. A new face for the old. Another page in the books of the zealots marching to die for their causes. Rid the world of the Infidels! Slay the Heretics! Butcher the Idolaters! Clean out the Nazis! Liquidate the crummy Red bastards!

I took a long, thoughtful turn around the sparkling fountain, and settled in a comfortable sidewalk café near the park where I watched the children and their parents.

I was burnt out. The cause had shifted from the German beasts to the Red Menace. Was it real? Of course it was real. England, the world, had another enemy, but for me, Duncan Reece, there had only been one—German Nazis.

They should not ask a man to have more than one cause in a lifetime. There were too many drops into the back fields of France and the Lowlands; too many silent, merciless murders; too many sad stories, too much of everything to ask a man to go through it all over again.

I had another drink and thought about Boyler's first visit to me in the Lion's Head. His red face slipped before my eyes and I could hear his drawling voice, his sarcastic, arrogant voice: "Is it our fault we didn't get the security we fought for? Or that you got mucked about afterwards? And not only you personally, but what has happened to the world in general? Duncan, my boy, we *had* to tell you to look for the end of the rainbow, what else did we have to offer you? We had our backs to the wall, and when you found out there was no rainbow, you rebelled...."

I sat in deep, dark silence in Marseille and watched the promenade on the boulevard and thought about my rebellion, which, ironically, had brought old-school-tie Philip Boyler to my pub door.

"… Now, if you are caught looting gambling tables and stripping beautiful women of their furs—no, I imagine furs would be too bulky—jewels certainly, and looting Ruden's safe, what could be more natural than your taking an envelope as you scooped up your other treasure? Who would suspect a common thief? And I have nothing to say about whatever else you might wish to make of your advantage. Matter of fact, the blacker your exploits, the more cover for us should you be caught.…"

All for the cause. The memory of the first one was too real. The memories remain. Very real. Many things I learned during those years remain with me still and force the memories on me. Little habits and cautions; double-tie your shoelace so it will not come undone and trip you; automatically check the entrances and exits of any room you enter; take care in shaving—a cut chin is another mark for identification by a witness. That is what makes the memories real.

I sat there and drank more raw cognac, listening to the city of Marseille around me, and thought about the Sentinel and his mission. Microfilm of blueprints. Astrophysical blueprints. They've torn up the Earth with their bombs, planes, tanks and guns. They ripped the green earth and made it ugly with the blood of men, and now they're reaching out into God's country.

I looked up into the clear Mediterranean sky. I had another drink and I stared into God's country, into the blue sky.

And then I settled back for some serious drinking.

12

It was raining. The sky was gray all over except for some heavy black over the Mediterranean Sea. I shaved, dressed and paid my hotel bill and rode in a cab until I found a restaurant I liked. I ate four eggs, more cheese and *café arrosé*. It was still raining after a second coffee with a lacing of rum.

I checked with the Italian brothers over the phone. Gino told me he and Marcus could leave the next day. I reminded him to have the Thompsons and ammo ready and wait for instructions. I hung up and stared through the window at the rain.

At ten minutes past ten I stood before the door of the bookshop rattling the latch. The blinds were pulled, but I noticed the slight movement to my left where someone had drawn back the torn and ripped curtain to see who it was.

The door opened and Hugh Roil, still in robe and slippers, peered at me. "It arrived an hour ago," he said. He handed me a letter. "Good luck." He closed the door.

I shoved the letter in my pocket and turned facing the street. Nothing but rain. I ducked my head against the downpour and went away from there quickly.

I walked in the rain for several blocks and stopped in a bistro with dirty, moist windows. A group of workers hung over a chessboard and did not bother to look up as I entered. I ordered cognac and settled in a corner near the door. I opened the letter. It was typewritten, with no heading and no signature.

Roger Delile is positively identified as a Red, and suggest, if he is in your way, to deal with him as you think best, as well as anyone you suspect connected with him. No information is available on the others. Apparently you have surrounded yourself with a scurvy crew from their records; but we can tie no Red associations to any of them. Move carefully against Delile, if you must move at all. He is a vital and valuable unit in their French activities, being in the Sûreté, with access to criminal records and the power to suppress or reveal damning evidence. Any move toward him will be highly suspect. Your query about Delile touched off an investigation that revealed him to be a Communist plant, so perhaps you can take some satisfaction from that. Ordinarily, we would notify the French, but their action against him might well connect you with us in the eyes of the Reds. Any move on Delile, then, must seem completely unofficial. He should die, if he must, as a policeman in the line of duty. This may be of use to you: Delile once used a bordello in the Montmartre as a hangout and general meeting place, and was on good terms with the woman who ran it, one Madame Molieûre; it is not known whether he still goes there, No. 32 Rue de la Cruix, but suggest you try to fit something into that picture. Nothing new has developed. Ruden's role, as well as his whereabouts, is still a mystery.

Delile. My vision blurred. I groped for the cognac and drank it quickly. I lit a cigarette. I read the letter again and struck a match to it. It curled into a fat flame and disappeared into black nothing.

It solved nothing. Only confirmed suspicions. If there was a connection between one of my men and Delile, something would happen in the future to prove it. I was absolutely sure my movements to Marseille and in that city for the last few days were without scrutiny. So Delile was a Red. Big help, Boyler. If you could have told me Tookie—or Otto—Saumur or one of the Della Vichias—was a Red it would have helped. But Delile …

I got up and slouched through the door and into the rain. I began to walk.

All right. Let's take it carefully and review: Delile is a Red and suspects you are in France for some other reason besides the answers you supplied him. I'm in France and I'm suspicious, what's the next step?

Find out what I'm doing here. How? Plant an agent.

Delile might operate, in his position, by nailing a guy for civil crimes. Catch a man and hold a gun to his head and make him work for you or turn him in. But who is it? Tookie? Otto? Saumur? Gino or Marcus?

Tookie would have had time to warn them of our proposed trip to southern France; Tookie had suggested Otto, he had suggested we stop at the De Mosel Inn where we picked up Saumur. He had suggested the Italian brothers.

Would Tookie act as Delile's agent? Considering that the U.S. Government in France didn't want any part of him, considering that Tookie had no friends and could get no help to fight Delile, he would. What did Tookie have to lose?

Tookie Smith had everything to gain … if there was a murder rap hanging over his head. The Le Havre fiasco. That story of his getting away had sounded too pat, too sure. Delile had apparently held Tookie on a string for a long time.

Okay, it's probably Tookie. But what happens if I cut Tookie down? Delile's pipeline of information is wiped out—and he moves in, like a good agent, taking no chances, and finishes me off. And they could finish me off.

I could do one of two things: Wait until the operation at the villa was over and I had the film—and then take care of Tookie (except that he might already have taken care of me)—or go to Paris and pay a personal call on one Monsieur le Inspector Roger Delile. And should anyone take Delile's place, it would give me time to go underground.

But what happens if Delile is cut out? Plenty, if the Party suspects that his sudden death has anything to do with this operation. Nothing at all if Delile is taken care of in the line of duty as an official of the Sûreté, as Boyler suggested.

I walked around some more in the rain and finally found the Gare de Paris and bought a first-class ticket to Paris on the Blue Train. It would not leave for another fifteen minutes, so I sat down beside a woman and a small child and lit a cigarette.

I smoked four cigarettes and concentrated on the water fountain and thought about absolutely nothing until the train was announced and I went aboard.

Once inside my compartment, I sat still as we made stops at Valence, Lyon, Dijon on the way to Paris, working out my plan for Delile. It would be a good tight plan. It would be in the line of duty. There might even be newspaper space about it.

13

After making sure Madame Molieûre was still the madame in No. 32 Rue de la Cruix, Montmartre, by the simple process of going to the big noisy house and having a drink with several of the girls, I hurried to complete the rest of my plan. It took me most of the day to find just the right place I would need. A small square near Place Pigalle was the hub for five streets, small winding alleyways and a busy boulevard. There were three Metro entrances and it was a junction for buses. A bistro was on each corner and along one block, facing onto the square, there was one sidewalk café after another. They faced the boulevard.

I rode past several times on different buses and toward evening had decided on the café with three streets and a Metro entrance within fifty feet of its doorway. Also, the cashier of the café was right beside the door.

I walked across the square and sat down at one of the tables and ordered wine. At about five-thirty, the buses began to roll into the junction more quickly and in succession. There was a factory area nearby and the workers began filling the cafés rapidly. At a quarter to six, I paid for my wine and got up slowly. I moved toward the Metro entrance and went inside with the press of crowds, allowing myself to be carried to the platforms. It would remain crowded like this for another half hour to forty-five minutes.

I did not like using the Metro for escape. But if I waited until dark, when I could scurry around in the alleys nearby, I would miss the Blue Train back to

Marseille. I would have to use the Metro—or the boulevard, which meant either a cab or stealing a car, which I did not want to do. It would have to be the Metro.

I glanced around the tracks, picking out the best place to cross, should I have to, and found a small opening at the end of the platform. It was just big enough for a man to squeeze through.

I went back up to the street level and into the nearest telephone booth. My hands were surprisingly steady as I dialed.

"I want to speak to Inspector Delile," I said to the voice that answered me, trying to imitate a Gascony accent.

"One moment." There was a series of clicks and buzzes.

"Yes?" he said. I recognized that voice immediately.

"M'sieu, I am calling for Madame Molieûre."

"Who?" He was being appropriately cautious.

"She has asked me to make this call, since she is very busy—I'm sure you'll understand—and to say she is returning a favor."

"I don't understand," he said quickly. "I'm very busy and—"

"Madame thought that a personal coup might help M'sieu in his already fine work at the Sûreté," I said, and then went on quickly, "today there were three men who came to the house. They were very drunk and talked a great deal. They are planning to rob the cashier at the Café Girondo at a quarter past six tonight when the café is filled with workers from the factory," I ended softly, in a whisper.

"Well, I will look into it," he said sharply, "but I know nothing of your Madame Molieûre. Goodbye." And then he hung up.

I stepped out of the booth and walked across the square and found a table inside the Café Girondo. I ordered Calvados and found my hand shaking as I brought it up to my lips. Delile was a cautious man, but I was certain his ignorance was as phony as it was convincing. I stared at the sidewalk before the door of the café, visualizing Delile, or myself, lying in a pool of blood.

I drank the Calvados quickly and ordered another.

I did have the advantage that I would see how many gendarmes he brought with him. I could see where they were placed and have that slight advantage. I looked at my watch. Five after six. They would be along in ten minutes. Ten minutes.

I gripped the butts of the two guns in my pockets tightly. It was reassuring to hold the hot metal in my hands and realize the power they represented.

The café began to crowd with tired old men who slumped into their chairs and ordered wine, talking in low tones, reading papers. It was an exceptionally hot day. I restrained a powerful urge to look at my watch again and kept my eyes on the street.

I saw him a moment later. He had come alone. He drove up to the other side of the square and stepped out and closed the door. He slipped his hand inside his jacket and loosened his gun and left his jacket open. He looked around. I followed his gaze. Two gendarmes came up out of the exit of the Metro and nodded in recognition to him. Delile looked in the opposite direction, and there again I saw two gendarmes moving slowly along the sidewalk toward the middle of the square.

I gripped the butts of the guns. Was he going to stand

outside and wait for the action to take place and attempt to make an arrest afterwards? I would be stopped cold if he did.

No. He began to move toward the café. Like a good cop, he was going to try and prevent a crime before it happened. I waited for him to get halfway across the square before I moved. I timed it so I would reach the cashier the moment he stepped onto the sidewalk before the door.

I moved slowly through the café and stopped at the cashier's to pay for the Calvados. I dropped money on the counter and turned toward the door. He was fifty feet away, eyes on me.

I turned suddenly and pulled the gun from my right pocket, the one he could see and jammed it in the cashier's face. "Stick-up." I snarled in French.

I saw him move out of the corner of my eye. He jammed his hand underneath his jacket. I pulled the gun from my left pocket and held it flat across my stomach. I don't think he saw it. I hit him four times in the chest before he jerked back across the curbstone and fell into the street. He was dead before he hit the ground.

All hell broke loose then. Men and women jumped out of their chairs and began to scream. The cashier fainted, falling onto the floor. Several men tried to grab me, but I showed them the two forty-fives and they fell back. I moved through the door, hitting the curbstone and moving past Delile in four strides. The gendarmes were rushing in on me.

The square was confusion. Screams, curses, whistles slashed through the air. Traffic stopped as if all power had been turned off. In a matter of seconds the quiet or orderly scene had been turned into a nightmare of hysteria.

I made for the Metro entrance. The two gendarmes from that side were coming in fast. I did not want to kill them. I got one in the leg and the other in the shoulder. They faded to the ground as I hit the Metro entrance. The knot of people around the steps dissolved away from me as I reached the first step at top speed.

Down in the tunnel a train was just pulling in. The people on the platform did not notice my running for the train. It was a common thing for that time of the evening. No one had heard the shots because of the noise the train made and I stood inside the car, staring around me, holding onto the two forty-fives deep in my pocket.

I got off at the next stop and raced to the street. I doubled back several blocks and found a cab. "Champs Élysées!" I said and settled back. I was not clear yet; I would not be clear until I had returned to south France.

I got out near the Rue le Marché and walked for more than two hours keeping to the shadows. I stripped my raincoat and hat, throwing them into a refuse basket, and continued walking, jamming the two guns into the waistband of my trousers.

I glanced at my watch—eight-thirty. I had an hour and a half before the train to Marseille left. Enough time to get another coat and find my way slowly to the station.

Enough time to be caught.

Hailing a cab, I rode over to the Left Bank and found a grubby second-hand clothing shop and bought an Argentine topcoat with deep side pockets. The little man locked the door behind me. I was the last customer for the night. It would be morning before he would make anything of my buying a coat, if by then. And in the morning I would be in Avignon—and Arles.

I arrived at the Gare de Lyon with ten minutes to spare. I had a double brandy, and stuffed sausage and bread into my mouth and washed it down with more brandy. Watching passengers move through the barrier to the Blue Train, I waited until five minutes to ten before dropping by the newsstand.

It was there all right. Just as I planned. On the front page of two papers, and with pictures of Delile in the street. A brave inspector had died in the line of duty when attempting to stop a holdup at the Café Girondo. Sûreté Inspector Delile had surprised the killer in the act of actually holding a gun on the Girondo's cashier.

From the descriptions given by the onlookers, there wasn't one chance in a thousand that they would identify me. The Party had lost their pipeline into the Sentinel's operation. The Party would believe what they read in the papers. And it would take time for the Party to make contact with their informant again— and I planned to watch Tookie, if it was Tookie.

Again I waited until the train began to move to make sure I was the last aboard. And I was.

I realized then that Boyler had managed to suck me in again.

I was involved with the Causes again.

The goddamn Causes.

Why is it, I argued with myself as the Blue Train sped past Melun, why is it that the cause you're supporting is always the right one?

It was just a question.

I didn't get an answer, possibly because I was asleep before the Blue Train, traveling at that same reckless speed, reached the other side of Melun.

14

That question gnawed at me again when I woke up. The train was pulling into Avignon. I could not find an answer but made a mental note to sit down some day and very quietly search for the reasoning behind the murders committed being sanctioned, while the murders committed against me were labeled inhuman crimes against society. Now was not the time for it.

Now was the time to get into Arles, rouse Tookie and Otto, make contact with Saumur in Montpellier and send a message to the Italians to stay put until I contacted them. If there were the slightest possibility of a repercussion from the Reds, it would culminate at Arles. I did not really believe that they could get back to me so quickly or easily. I was sure I had broken up the key to their pattern, but that interminable caution checked my confidence.

I had decided not to mention the Delile death until the opportune moment arose. If there was justification to my suspicions of Tookie, he would make an effort to contact Delile again. And that would be the moment to present him with the facts.

I arrived in Avignon before 7:00 A.M. and took a cab over to Arles. An hour later, I called Tookie and Otto and told both of them to get out of their hotels at once and start walking the main road toward Montpellier. I then called Saumur. He said he had gotten the six new tires without difficulty and would leave immediately, being on the lookout for Tookie and Otto. Gino was not available and I spoke to Marcus. I impressed on him the necessity of being ready to move out when I sent for them. He said he would give the message to Gino.

I lighted a cigarette and studied the heavy rain outside the phone booth. I was tired. The sleep on the train down from Paris had not been restful. My mouth was stale and I wanted a hot bath and solid breakfast before bed. I settled for a quick cup of coffee at a nearby counter and turned to the rainswept road to Montpellier.

It might have been an hour later, a few miles outside Arles toward the village of St. Giles, that Saumur hove around a curve and into view. He splashed to a stop. Otto and Tookie sat in the back of the car amid the boxes of food the big Frenchman had bought in Marseille.

"Turn the car around—back to Montpellier," I said, getting in beside him. "And slow down." He turned the car around. "Any more trouble with the gendarmes?" I asked him.

"No, *mon ami*. As the boss ordered, I sat in the hotel, and I sat very still except for getting the tires."

"You two have any trouble?" I asked, turning around to look at Tookie and Otto. Both of them were soaked to the skin. There had been no trouble. Otto had learned nothing about the Ruden bazaar. There was no talk. I agreed with him that it was a little early for street gossip with the affair still two weeks away.

"We need a house," I said to Saumur. "You know this country. An abandoned farm, a big house, or barn, or warehouse. Anything we can train in without trouble."

"Training!" Otto's voice was full of respect. "We are going to train for this mission. That is good. *Ja!*"

"Well?" I asked Saumur.

His face was screwed up tight in thought. "North of

Lunel, there is an old man who owns a grain mill. It is a big building. And he lives alone."

"How far is it from Arles?"

"Forty kilometers."

"About twenty-five miles," I said. "That should do it. Is it isolated?"

"*Comment?*"

"How far to the nearest neighbor?"

"There is no one around for several kilometers, with clear fields on all sides. One can easily see when the house is being approached. I know it well, having worked for a cattle breeder in Nimes who used to buy grain from him."

"That's it then," I said simply. "Let's go." I spun around in my seat. Tookie's face was drained white. He began to cough. "Did you get those small-scale maps?" I asked Otto.

"Right here, boss," he replied, and handed them over. "Where did you pick up the topcoat?" Tookie asked me.

"Why?" I opened the maps.

"Just asking. That's a funny cut. Never saw one like it before."

"In Paris," I said, looking at him. "Last night."

"Paris!" he frowned. "You were in Paris last night?" I didn't answer.

"We cut off here," Saumur said, and turned sharply to the right, up a small muddy track that began to wind upward. To the left of us, in the distance through the haze and mist of the slackening rain, I could see the church steeples of Lunel. The road was muddy and Saumur had to drive carefully.

Along another road, far to the right, we could see a man walking in back of a hay rick. If he saw us, he didn't bother to change the position of his head.

Tookie continued to cough. Otto opened a bottle of wine and gave it to him, but it didn't do much good. "I gotta get dry clothes on and get warmed up," Tookie said to me. "My chest feels like it's on fire."

"How much further?" I asked Saumur.

"A little more." replied the Frenchman.

"Gimme your jacket, sweetheart," Tookie said, patting Saumur on the shoulder. I held the wheel while Saumur slipped out of the thick woolen jacket and handed it back to Tookie. He drank more wine and huddled up in the corner.

I opened the maps full and began studying them. He had bought four maps of the southern districts near Arles, favoring the Spanish border. There were Gard, Hérault, Aude and Pyrenees-Orientales. I traced down the roads with my eye, working out a preliminary escape route from Arles, bypassing Montpellier and Narbonne, on good roads, one through Séte on the coast and another through Carcassonne further to the west. But I did not like the idea of going so far west and made a note to explore thoroughly the countryside for a second route without having to rely on Carcassonne. Once over the border we would head directly to Barcelona. All that remained was to figure out a way of getting past the border check points, which shouldn't prove too difficult. As Tookie had said, there should be a zillion cuts through those lousy Pyrenees.

Saumur's sudden swerving of the car detracted my attention from the maps. He had pulled off the slick muddy road into a shaded lane of firm soil and grass. I could see the wide fields he mentioned. And up ahead, a house, several smaller buildings and a huge two-storied fieldstone building, with a pitched roof and battened windows, that would be perfect for our training.

A dog came from around the house when we pulled into the yard and started barking, followed in a moment by a shrunken, shriveled old man bent over at the shoulders from years of heavy work. He wore the boots of a field man and his leather fleece-lined jacket was slick and still not dried from the rain. He carried a pitchfork.

"Bon Soir," Saumur said heartily, and opened the door.

"What do you want?" asked the old man suspiciously. He remained standing. Saumur walked over to him. "Eh, what do you want?"

"We want your house, old man," said Saumur with a grin.

"Who are you? What do you say now? You want to use my house, eh?"

"That's the truth," Saumur said. The old man stepped back and raised the pitchfork.

"I haven't any money!" the old man cried. "I put all my money in the Lunel bank!"

Saumur reached out suddenly and grabbed the pitchfork and twisted it easily out of the old man's hand, breaking it over his knee. The old man turned to run, but Saumur was on him quickly. He pinned the old man's hands behind his back easily in one large fist.

"I gotta get outa here," said Tookie in back of me, his teeth chattering. He opened the door and hurried into the cottage. Saumur pushed the old man toward the door, with Otto and myself following.

It was warm inside. The lime-washed walls were inviting and the room comfortable to look at. There was a fair-sized kitchen, two large bedrooms with double beds in each and a stepladder leading to the garret beneath the room. I climbed the ladder while Saumur sat the old man down in a chair and Tookie crowded in on the hearth. Otto searched the house methodically and, jerking his thumb outside with a nod at me, went to explore the other buildings.

I came downstairs and shucked out of my wet coat. Saumur tied the old man and then turned to the fire where Tookie was stripping down to the skin. "Get the car out of sight," I said to Saumur.

Tookie had rummaged around for clothes and came up with a faded pair of trousers, heavy woolen sweater and work jacket by the time Saumur and Otto returned. "The grain building is empty. And there is a lot of room in it for most anything," Otto reported.

I nodded. "Otto, you're on first guard. Everybody stands guard six hours on and eighteen off. Remember who follows you. When the Italians show up, we'll stretch it out to four on and twenty off."

"The top floor of the grain building would make an excellent sentry post," Otto said. "The windows are battened, but I can make peep holes."

"Okay," I said. "We'll get the walkie-talkies out in a little while—you can warn us down here if anyone comes up the road."

I sent Saumur to rig the talkies and turned to Tookie. "You cook the first meal. We take turns at that, too."

"Sure, boss," he said and began opening closets.

As I brought the food and gear from the car into the house, I thought about The Sentinel and the motivation behind the logistics, preparation and care of the operation, with something of a shudder for the future. Tomorrow I would send Saumur into Marseille to get Gino and Marcus, then we would begin.

Tookie was frying onions in fresh butter. I looked up. He was moving about the kitchen as if he had been there all his life. I thought about Delile. If my suspicions of Tookie were grounded in fact, and he was a pipeline into Delile's office, then with Delile out of the way, I could breathe easier. And even if he wasn't, at least I felt confident it would take time for the Reds to get someone to take Delile's place and reestablish contact with my operation, and that would give me the breathing space and time I needed.

I turned to the problem of making out a list of the equipment we would need. Coveralls—we would all wear the same clothes. Sneakers—I would have to get shoe sizes. Nylon—for rope ladders that we could weave....

15

It continued to rain for two days, the entire time Saumur was in Marseille locating the list of gear and picking up the two Italians. Tookie was unable to move from the roaring fire he kept going day and night, wrapped in a thick woolen comforter, baking one side and then the other, fighting the damp chill the continuous rain brought into the house. Otto and I split guard duty in the grain building.

Two miserable days in which I brooded over my predicament. I went through a succession of periods filled with indecision and doubt; hatred for Boyler and the mission; loathing for my weakness at not being able to resist the temptation of money; anger and fury at the world political situation that reduced me to a nameless digit again—and made me kill again.

I stopped it when I began to argue seriously with myself about life, and drowned the bleakness and the stark pictures in a bottle of wine. I felt only a little better when I came out of it—but more adjusted to the situation.

I was respectful too, once the momentary bitterness was over, of the desperateness of my position now that the Reds might be forced to use more ambitious plans against me. But even here, when I began to force my thinking along lines they might use, my mind bogged down into a morass of conflicting doubts, uncertainty and fear.

About nine in the evening of the third night I spotted a car pulling into the farm road and called Otto on the talkie. In seconds I heard the door open below me and knew Otto had taken a position covering the yard and the road. While I was expecting Saumur, and I recognized the car, I could not afford to take chances. When I heard Saumur's big voice bellow a greeting, I went below and met him and the Italians.

Marcus had gotten out of the car first and was stretching dramatically. "Very good! Excellent!" he said slowly, nodding approval as he glanced around the farm. He walked into the house.

I waited until he got halfway through the door before calling him back. "Help us get this gear inside."

He did not move. Gino spoke to him in Italian. The older brother looked around quickly. "Good spot, boss," he said with a brief smile. "Saumur tells me we're going to make dummy runs and practice for the job."

"He likes the idea," Saumur said, pulling out the heavy cartons from the rear of the car and stacking them on the ground.

"It's sensible," Gino shrugged and picked up one of

the boxes. Marcus looked at me with vicious eyes and followed his brother into the house with the smallest box.

Saumur grinned. "He—"

"Inside," I said, before he could speak, and grabbed the boxes.

Inside, Marcus was standing before the fireplace warming himself and talking rapidly to Gino in Italian. His brother tasted a glass of wine cautiously. I dropped the box on the floor and looked around the room. This was the first time we had all been together. They looked at me expectantly.

I lit a cigarette to see if my hand was shaking. It wasn't. I walked across the room and faced Marcus. I stood six inches away from him. "When I give you an order," I said as evenly as I could, "you do what I tell you. You don't turn to Gino for approval. You take my orders or get out, now."

Gino put the wine glass down carefully and turned his back on Marcus. Otto, Saumur and Tookie stood behind me. They were silent. Waiting. "You are the boss," Marcus said softly. A little too dramatically.

"You're goddamned right I'm the boss." I said. "And don't forget it."

"You are the boss," he repeated, a trace of insolence in his voice. "The boss."

"And don't forget it," I insisted.

"I won't forget it." He tried, but he did not succeed in not glancing at his brother.

"That's settled," I announced, turning to look at all of them. "And it damn well better be settled once and for all."

But I knew it wasn't settled. Marcus' kind had to be shown. So far it was nothing but words. And Gino was the one I would eventually have to go up against.

I set the guard duty in the grain building and explained the walkie-talkie to them. "And the only time you use it is when someone or something is coming or there is trouble. No personal messages—no chit-chat. Strictly business. At night, we turn the volume of the big radio set up loud. All you do is speak."

Gino was first on guard. He nodded, hefted one of the Thompsons and followed Saumur out of the door. Otto, Tookie and myself began emptying the boxes of gear. Marcus stood to one side waiting for orders. "Get into the kitchen and clean it up. It's messy now, because we haven't had time to clean it up. But from now on, whoever cooks, cleans." I turned to opening the boxes.

There was nearly a half-dozen of everything I ordered. Wire cutters, heavy leather gloves and skin-tight silk ones. Pencil flashlights with spare bulbs and batteries; several spools of medical tape, industrial tape and four hundred feet of seven-hundred-pound test nylon rope with fourteen-inch-spread grappling hooks. There were tubes of black theatrical makeup and black Basque type berets that could be pulled low over the forehead. Three wrist watches with sweep second hands, one each for Tookie, Saumur and Otto, who did not have watches. Several yards of black cloth for handkerchief masks, a half-dozen flat steel jimmy tools, a twenty-five-gallon gasoline can to be filled and taken with us, three bottles of good brandy for crossing the mountains into Spain. On and on, everything I could think of, or that Tookie, Saumur or Otto could think of that we would need for the raid on the villa.

"What do we do tomorrow?" Otto asked when he had finished sorting and stripping identification tags and labels from the gear.

"We begin," I replied simply. "You three go to bed. I want to check outside before I turn in."

Saumur and Otto turned to the second bedroom while Tookie spread his comforters before the hearth and banked the fire. Marcus had finished his cleanup of the kitchen and gone to bed without a word to any of us.

The rain left it crisp outside in the dark. I stood still until I could make out the familiar objects in the yard before walking toward the grain building. I thought I had heard it when I stepped outside, but it wasn't until I got my foot on the step that I knew I heard it. A car, possibly on the main road. I hurried upstairs to find Gino crouched before one of the peepholes in the wood-battened windows.

"Is it turning into our road?" I asked.

"Gone on past." Gino shook his head.

"Did it stop at all—or even slow down?"

"I don't think so. It was going pretty steady," Gino said.

"Someone could have jumped from a moving car," I said. "Better be careful—and warn Marcus when he relieves you," I said, straining my eyes in the darkness.

Gino straightened up. "Who knows we're here?"

I thought about that a moment. "It could be friends of the old man's, maybe. He could have habits we don't know about. Maybe he's missed. Friends might come to investigate and see if he's sick."

"And jump from a moving car?" he asked.

I didn't answer. "Good night," I said and returned to the farmhouse, sprawling on the bed beside Marcus. He was curled up on one side of the bed like a baby. He even looked like a baby.

16

"Boss! Boss! Wake up!"

I fought my way through a curtain of heavy sleep and struggled to my feet. Otto was shaking me by the shoulder. "What—what is it?"

"The old man has escaped. Marcus fell asleep on guard."

He turned and ran out of the doorway and into the farmyard. The sun was just a slight yellow pip rising above the rim of the far meadow as I staggered through the door. Tookie, Saumur, Gino and Marcus were scurrying around the outer buildings looking for the old man.

"Get the car," I snapped at Otto. "Tookie, Saumur, Gino!"

They stopped their search and ran toward me. Gino was still in shorts and barefoot. "Spread out— Tookie, take the left, Saumur the rear of the house, with Gino on the right. I'll take the car with Otto and—" I stopped. Marcus ran up breathless.

"You stay here!" I said as harshly as I could. "Get inside and stay there until we get back. And for your sake, I hope we find that old man."

Saumur and Tookie had already spun away and were loping through the fields and beating the hedges, dropping down into ditches. Gino had disappeared into a thick tangle of brush and trees, throwing himself into it unmindful of the fact he was dressed only in shorts.

Otto threw the door open for me and slipped over while I got under the wheel of the car. "Keep your eyes open in the hedges," I said. "If we don't get him in fifteen minutes, we might as well keep going," I said bitterly. "What happened back there?"

"I went to check the old man in the garret." Otto said coldly, "and found he had slipped his ropes. I ran up to check with Marcus and found him asleep."

"On the floor, or standing up?" I demanded.

There was a trace of open contempt in Otto's voice. "He was stretched flat on the floor, the gun leaning against the wall."

I hit the road leading to the main highway with my foot all the way down on the accelerator. I slammed on the brakes. "I'll take it right, you left. Don't shoot unless you absolutely must."

Otto nodded grimly, swung out of the door and was running down the road, ranging from side to side searching the hedges and ditches before I could get the car in gear.

I moved quickly along the road, my mind racing. If he wanted help, it would be wisest, I thought, to try for the main highway and stop a car. He might still be within range if I could get to the main highway before him.

I was on that highway a few minutes later and began patrol at a speed that would allow me to search the hedges and trees on either side. I drove three miles either side of the cutoff and not a sign of him. If he had gotten through to Lunel, we wouldn't have more than an hour to get packed and clear out.

Cursing Marcus for everything I could think of, I whipped the car around and drove as fast as I could back to the farm.

They were waiting for me when I drove up. They had the old man.

"Where was he?" I asked Otto, who held him by the rm.

"Hiding in a hedge."

"Did you see anyone? Talk to anyone?" I demanded, facing the old man.

His jaw quivered. His clothes were covered with muddy slime. He shook his head. "No one," he whispered.

"If anyone comes here, old man," I said, "you will see your house and barn burned to the ground—before we kill you."

"I swear—before merciful heaven—that I saw no one, M'sieu." He would have sagged to the ground if Otto had not held him up.

"Take him inside and see that he's tied properly," I said to Otto. I turned around and faced Marcus, watching Gino out of the corner of my eye. He was about eight feet from me and watching every move I made.

He carried the Thompson machine gun.

"I'll shoot you between the eyes if you step out of line once more, Marcus," I said with restraint, but not enough to keep my voice from quivering.

His lip curled. He tried to pull the forty-five from his coverall pocket. I chopped down hard on his wrist. The gun dropped to the ground. I brought up a right hand and caught him behind the ear. He staggered back, eyes tightening up and burning at me. He stooped to pick up the gun and I kicked him in the face. He went backward and over on his side.

"*Leave him alone*," Gino said.

I spun around to one side and dove for the spot where I knew Gino was. The Thompson was leveled at my back. Even as I was flying through the air, I saw his finger tighten on the trigger.

A terrible noise exploded in my ears.

17

I clawed the ground, the echoes reverberating in my ears, and somehow caught hold of what had to be Gino's legs. I pulled hard. Something fell backward.

Something else hit me on the head.

I opened my eyes. Gino was chopping at me with the gun, fighting me off. Suddenly the chopping stopped just as it was beginning to get through to me that I wasn't going to take much more of that.

I looked up. Otto had the gun and was backing up. Saumur was holding Marcus. Gino was on his feet, stepping in, swinging for my head. I caught most of it on my head and rolled over—I rolled over again and came up on my feet.

I faced him, staggering backward away from him. I shook my head and fought to keep from rubbing my aching head. Marcus was screaming at his brother in Italian.

Gino moved in slowly, his face showing nothing, eyes steady and hands outstretched, shoulders hunched forward, head pulled in like a wrestler.

I backed up more, stalling for time until my head cleared. "He was wrong, Gino," I gasped.

He didn't reply. One hand extended a little further than the other, one foot trailing the other, he moved in on me.

"How long are you going to take up for him?" I wheezed. "His letting the old man get away could have cost us everything."

He blinked his eyes.

"There's only room for one boss," I said. I risked a glance at the others. Tookie, Saumur and Otto watched me with impassive expressions. "How about it, Gino?" I asked. My head was clearing. "You're making his trouble your trouble."

"He's my brother," Gino said. "Right or wrong, he's my brother."

I moved in while he was talking, my mouth suddenly going dry, my mind riddled with crazy thoughts. I hit him hard in the face. But he took it well and lunged in for me as I expected he would.

I grabbed that outstretched hand and twisted it with every ounce of strength I had. I got it behind him and pulled up on it. I chopped him on the neck with my free hand. He went down, face first into the dirt.

He got up quickly, choking for breath, his face full of mud, and made a lunge for me. I brought my knee up quickly and caught him in the pit of the stomach and, when he slumped over, chopped him on the neck again.

Marcus had stopped screaming.

Gino lunged at me from a sitting position. I sidestepped and let him fall headlong into the grass and mud, straddled him quickly and rapped him a half dozen times on the neck. He turned blue and began to struggle for breath, then slumped out cold.

I turned toward Marcus. "Let him go."

Saumur let him go. He stood still, looking at Gino on the ground. "He won't fight for you anymore," I said. "Either take orders, or I'll kill you."

Marcus spoke to his brother in Italian. Gino was struggling to a sitting position. "Ask him," I said. "Ask him if he will fight for you again."

Marcus spoke to him in Italian again.

"I told you," Gino said with difficulty, "I told you—one of these days you would have to start looking out for yourself."

Marcus said something in Italian.

Gino shook his head. "I've done all I can. But I won't kill him for you and that's the only thing left."

Gino got up and staggered toward the house.

Marcus looked at me and started after his brother. He caught him at the door and tried to help him, but the older brother tore free, and screaming at him in Italian, slapped Marcus viciously across the face. He disappeared into the house.

"Go on guard, Otto," I said. "Tookie, you and Saumur start weaving that rope ladder. Soon as Gino is okay, we start training."

"*Oui*," Saumur grunted.

Otto picked up Marcus' gun, his blue eyes glistening and walked over to where Marcus stood beside the house. He handed him the gun and walked away. Marcus looked at the gun and at me, then put it in his pocket and went into the house.

Tookie stepped beside me. "Boss," he said gently, "that was as sweet a piece of work as I ever saw. But I want you to know, there's only one way it coulda gone."

"Why, Tookie?" I asked.

He said slowly: "I watched you and him and all I could think about was your mission. Get that! Not about the money—just what kind of an operation you're on. You never briefed me on that, sweetheart. You oughta think about it in case something happens to you."

"Nothing's going to happen to me," I said.

"Okay, sweetheart, if that's the way you want it."

"That's the way it's going to be," I said.

"Sure, sure," he chuckled, his eyes remote and thoughtful. "But don't hold your cards so close to your face they scrape meat off." He turned and walked toward the house where Saumur was uncoiling the rope.

18

I had been in France sixteen days. That left me ten days to work them into a tight, efficient unit, dependable and capable of striking quickly and effectively and then, getting away.

Ten days.

We began that afternoon with light exercises. The first day was difficult, the second harder still and the third a screaming terror as our little-used muscles, sprained joints and blistered hands rebelled. Tookie was absolutely incapable of going on after the second day. Any extended physical exercise sent him into a paroxysm of coughing. By the sixth day we had all thinned down a bit and I was amazed and proud of myself the morning we started the last four days of training, concentrating on coordinated movements against the grain building, using the grappling hook to swing up to the roof and then climbing the rope ladder. Morale was high. The trouble with Marcus was forgotten and both Gino and Marcus worked long and hard. I was the undisputed leader; they accepted it and I expected nothing less than that acceptance.

I was constantly on the alert for the right moment to mention Delile's death, and more than once I nearly blurted it out. But none of them, especially Tookie, whom I had relieved of his guard duty because of his coughing and had watched constantly, had made any kind of a move I could honestly interpret as being out of the ordinary.

Late in the afternoon we had knocked off for a cigarette and coffee and the conversation drifted to what we would do with our share of the Ruden loot. I was struck with the similarity of their views and attitudes. Everyone of us had been directly and deeply affected by war. To the man, their values were similar to my own, and for nearly the same reasons. Cynical, mistrustful, bitter, but, surprisingly, not defeated.

Gino spoke of his life in America with his father and the hopes the Senor Della Vichia had held for a uniting of the family. Leaving his mother and little Marcus in Italy after the first World War, Papa Della Vichia had hoped for a good life for his family. After establishing himself in Brooklyn, he had returned to Italy and had been forced to remain by the Mussolini Fascists. Marcus had never known any other way of life except the Black Shirts. Gino had been left alone in the States and, during the Thirties and Forties, had inevitably turned to crime. "Live dangerously! That's what that fat bastard told them," Gino jeered. He uttered a four-letter word. "You know how many poor, stupid wops fell for that? Everyone of them. And my brother one of the biggest. He thought sleeping with another man's wife was living dangerously!"

He got up and lit a cigarette. "I'm cutting out for Mexico. Buy a nice little restaurant-gin mill combination and become another wop with a spaghetti joint. Maybe even a wife and kids—I never tried that before. This is about the last chance I'll get for heavy folding stuff."

Otto was just as bitter about his side of the war. His

background was different, but his values were the same, his dreams along the same lines. "I really didn't know about Dachau and Buchenwald—" He stopped and closed his eyes. "When I saw the ovens, I think I died. Or perhaps I began to live."

"I saw those ovens," Tookie said in a harsh metallic voice.

Otto did not notice. "I plan a big ranch in Argentina," he continued. "A big ranch where I can raise cattle and sell them to the Russians and the Americans when they start the next war."

"*Sacrê bleu!*" Saumur said disgustedly. "You made war, your people," growled the big Frenchman. "In the history they will write about it, *mon ami*, the political passions will be forgotten—just as the passions of the War of the Roses are forgotten. So, I think maybe I will join you on that ranch in Argentina and sell cattle for the next war. I know all there is to know about cattle, eh?"

Otto raised up one arm and looked at the Frenchman, his eyes clear and blue beneath the shading fingers. "I will think about it, Jean Saumur," he said slowly. "*Ja!* I will think about it."

"How about you, Tookie?" I asked.

"Back to the States for me. Arizona. I gotta get rid of this rattle in my chest before I can make other plans."

"Marcus," volunteered Gino reflectively, "will probably go with me."

"And you, boss?" asked Saumur. "What happens to you?"

"Respectability," I said. "Back to London as a middle-class merchant."

I thought about that the rest of the afternoon. That import-export license was the dream. But what about reality? You're a different man, Reece, from when you first started thinking for yourself. A man who has no principles, as ascribing to no morality, who has perhaps had the morality knocked out of you. You're a killer; a procurer and thief; a man who has great wit and wisdom when it comes to saving your own neck and feathering your nest. You see that the world is mad and are playing along with it.

Can such a man slip into the comfortable rut of middle-class merchant?

Another question.

And no answer for it.

19

That evening I decided on who would handle the specific jobs. Tookie and I had proved to be the most agile at climbing the rope ladder and hooking on with the grappler. We would be the roof men. Otto and Marcus would pair off and hide in the river weeds several days before the bazaar. Gino and Saumur, physically the strongest, would be sent in from the front to deal with the guards at the gate and the chauffeurs, as well as to disable the automobiles.

After another day of intense training, Saumur and I left to inspect the roads on escape routes I had marked out. Inspecting each turn in the road carefully and marking it on the map as to how fast the curve could be taken, we toured a direct, as well as two alternate routes, using side roads when possible, but making sure they would take heavy speeds. While the distance between Arles and our destination of Port-Vendres, the last French village on the Spanish border, was relatively small, roughly a hundred miles, I refused to take unnecessary chances. In Beziers we filled the gasoline can and stored it in a small wood on the outskirts of Narbonne.

We made a deal with Vieliéz Costa, a gnarled little Spaniard, to take us across the mountains to Port Pou in Spain and, after much haggling done only to convince him that we were poor smugglers, I paid over half of his price. He would meet us in Port-Vendres the morning following the raid and assured us he knew not one, but more than a dozen secret passages across the impasse into Spain. I don't think he believed our story about smuggling, but I could tell he didn't care one way or the other.

Skirting Lunel, we returned to the farm twenty-four hours later to find Tookie practicing with the rope ladder while Otto, Marcus and Gino tape-tied one another's wrists again and again. I called them together and told them to start packing Otto's and Marcus' gear. Saumur would drive the two to Nimes, where they would take a bus to the outskirts of Arles.

I briefed them for the last time before they drove away. "Hide in the weeds and do not move about under any circumstances," I said. "We will make contact with you at exactly ten o'clock on the evening of the bazaar over the talkie."

Otto listened to me, his clear blue eyes bright and hard. He must have been a magnificent soldier. Marcus was eager and enthusiastic. "Otto is the leader of the group," I said to him. "You take his orders. He is well-trained and you can depend on him."

"I understand," Marcus said quietly.

"More than likely there will be guards posted in advance of any arrivals by guests. Try to establish how many there are and where they are positioned." Otto nodded that he understood.

"We will go by group names. Tookie and I will be group one—Saumur and Gino group two—Marcus and Otto group three. Remember, no names."

Otto repeated the instructions back to me carefully. And then, with their gear checked and packed in rucksacks, they got into the car. Saumur got under the wheel and started the engine. Gino walked to the car and spoke gently in Italian to his brother, then kissed him affectionately on the cheek. Otto stared stonily ahead.

"Hang around Arles tonight," I said to Saumur, "not more than a few hours, and see what you can pick up in the cafés. Any talk or information about the villa or the guards. We'll expect you back here by midnight."

"*Oui*," grunted the big Frenchman, and nodded.

Tookie clapped Otto on the shoulder. "Give'm hell, kraut! When this is over, I'll buy you a long tall one in Arizona."

"*Auf Wiedersehen*, Tookie!" Otto said with a smile. "*Auf Wiedersehen*, boss."

"*Arrivederci*," Gino said to them.

"Good luck!" I called to them as the car rolled out of the yard. We watched until they disappeared off the farm road.

20

Saumur returned on time with news that the entire city of Arles was buzzing with the coming bazaar. The hotels were packed, the cafés filled with more celebrities driving up from the Riviera or coming from

Paris, New York and London in specially chartered planes. From as far away as Rio de Janeiro and Hollywood, there were planes scheduled to arrive with guests. And the streets were swarming with plainclothes Sûreté.

The night before we were to pull out, I had a straight six-hour guard from midnight until six in the morning. My idea was to sleep some in the morning and leave the farm about three in the afternoon. I was pacing the floor of the grain building thinking over the hundreds of things that might occur and then trying to figure out ways to meet them, when I heard a noise.

The cows were inside for the night, and I knew none of the others would be up. We slept every spare minute we could. I thought about the old man.

I turned to the talkie and started to press the button for a call to the farmhouse and a check on the old man when I heard it again. I released the button and pulled the forty-five.

Slipping out of the building softly, I moved across the yard and into the house. The moon had dropped an hour before and it was that inky black period just before dawn. Gino, Saumur and Tookie were asleep. I checked the old man in the garret. He was snoring loudly, and tied down.

I heard it again. A squeaking that was a familiar sound but that I could not place.

The window! Someone was trying to open the window to one of the bedrooms.

I slipped out of the house and moving slowly, crouched low, skirted wide and came up in back of him. I slipped forward and brought the gun down hard on his head. He slumped to the ground without a sound.

One of the sleepers inside the room groaned. I ducked

down, breathing tightly. It was Saumur, grumbling in his sleep.

I searched the man and found what I was looking for and nothing else—a wallet with a thick wad of French francs. No cards, no identification. An Italian stiletto was slipped snugly inside his boot top.

I got him under the armpits and dragged him back to the grain room, having to carry him across my shoulders to get him up the stairs. I used his own belt and shoe laces to tie him up and stuffed my handkerchief in his mouth. I flashed a light on him.

He was dressed like the four in the Lyon wood. Black suit, white shirt, black tie. I examined the seams of his clothes and tore his shoes apart. There was no identification.

I pressed my thumbs against his eyeballs. After a little of that he came out of it. I slapped his face a few times to wake him up fully and yanked the handkerchief out of his mouth. I pressed the stiletto against the bare instep of his right foot. "Talk, M'sieu, and it had better be the right kind of talk."

No answer.

I pressed the point of the stiletto a little harder and brought blood. He flinched, but he took it. "Who sent you? Who were you after?"

"You cannot torture me enough to make me talk," he said in guttural French.

"That may be so, M'sieu," I said, "but in that case, I will just kill you." I pressed the stiletto harder. He jerked his foot back. "Who sent you? Who were you after?"

He closed his eyes and then opened them.

"Were you trying to kill me?" I asked.

He stared at me.

"Were you trying to contact someone?"

He closed his eyes. I reached over and slapped his face hard. He glared at me a moment, then the eyes faded.

"What were your instructions from the Party?"

That didn't get anything either.

"Are you a member—or just a hired hand?" I asked, and lit a cigarette. He watched every movement I made.

"Do you know who I am?"

He didn't answer. I placed the end of the cigarette against his little toe. He jerked back.

"Let me show you the picture, M'sieu," I said. "We are in an old building far away from any help." I took a deep drag on the cigarette, sat down on the floor before him and blew smoke in his face. "You certainly know that I am an intelligence agent. Plans have been made—big plans—with much money and people involved—and at the cost of lives—five, so far, fortunately all of them from your side. You come to kill me—or contact someone in my party."

He stared at me. He was thinking.

"Are you with me, M'sieu? I hope you are, because I am about to make my point. I don't know you. You are a zero to me. You represent a very real threat to my life. Why would I hesitate, M'sieu, to kill you, if I thought you would harm me or my mission? Answer me, M'sieu."

"I know nothing," he said. But he was thinking about it. The eyes softened.

"How did you get here? How did you know about this place?"

"I received orders on the telephone."

"Who sent them to you?"

"I do not know. I receive my orders under a prearranged plan. I do not question the orders. I do as instructed."

"And your instructions?"

"How do I know you will not kill me after I tell you?" he asked.

"M'sieu, that is the game, *n'est-ce pas?*"

"A man's life is not a game," he said.

"No, certainly not my life, M'sieu. There is no guarantee. I am sorry. You must tell me what you know and take your chances."

"And if I don't, you kill me?"

"Certainly."

"And if I do?" He shrugged. "*Oui*, that is the game." He took a deep breath. "I am a brick mason."

"A Party member?"

"*Oui*. Last night I received a telephone call. I was told a parcel would be in the locker of the bus station at No. 7 Garibaldi Boulevard in Marseille. I went there to that place and found these clothes, a wallet with money and a printed note telling me to come to this farm and, with the stiletto that was in the parcel, kill everyone here."

"And the note, M'sieu?"

"I destroyed it," he said, and stared at me.

I lit another cigarette. "How will you explain the failure of your mission, M'sieu, if I let you go?"

Real terror flashed in his eyes. He cursed softly. "You are a devil, M'sieur!"

"When I complete my mission, they will know that you have failed. What will they do to you, eh?"

He uttered an oath—then changed it quickly to a prayer. I believed him. The pattern was well known. Terror if they refused to obey orders; terror if they failed in their mission; an even worse terror if they were successful, with the threat of exposing you if you did not follow orders from then on. I dragged him to the ground floor of the grain building and deposited him in back of some grain bags.

"You can live three or four days without water. If I am successful in my mission, I will tell the police. They will come release you. That is the best I can do, M'sieu."

He stared at me, then his face twisted in a sudden grimace of pain. His body shook and he relaxed.

"M'sieu?" I said in a voice that sounded like someone else's. "M'sieu?" I dropped down beside him. I had seen this once before.

He was dead.

I saw a soldier drop dead of a heart attack during the war. The soldier's face had twisted agony on it a second before death.

Now I had seen it twice.

The sky was just beginning to get that dirty blue look just before the sun breaks through over the east. I went back into the house and made a pot of coffee. I took a cup and saucer down from the cupboard and poured a cup, then took the pot with me and, sat on the front door step watching the sun come up full.

My guilt and fears caught up with me this time. This made the score six for me, none for them. You can't ignore your conscience too hard for too long. It catches up with you and begins to squeeze you dry, withers your heart and puts ice in your veins instead of blood, and you get old before your time.

That's what happens when you do it alone. In war there's a difference. There is method. During war, they had convinced me my precious identity would be returned intact, that the anonymity I suffered was really protection against myself. My conscience, they said, would be restored when my true self was returned from National Service, when I reemerged from the nameless in war. I was not to think in terms of individual crimes against humanity. If that were so, they said, they would have a hysterical mass of thirty millions wandering around feeling guilty. The Nation and the Cause were solely responsible.

I sat on the steps drinking coffee, smoking, watching a sun rise, and coldly, with chilling isolation, cut my conscience right out and did not think any more of the dead man behind the grain sacks.

I went inside and woke each of them up. "We're moving out!"

They got up and dressed quickly without a word. We loaded the rucksacks into the car and checked and rechecked the house for anything left behind. Once inside the car, I ordered Tookie to go cut the old man's leg ropes. He would be able to manage well enough if he could walk and it would give us plenty of time.

Saumur drove. "We need a hideout for the rest of the day," I said, my voice tired and ragged. "Any place where there are a lot of trees and protection."

"*Oui!*" he said. "I know a place."

I was tired and cranky and guilty and frightened, and all within myself. I was not amoral. I was an ordinary human being with a cause that I *had* to believe was above everything or lose the shaky grasp on what little reality there was left for me to live with and understand.

Concentrate now—concentrate on the operation. Concentrate on the villa, the guards, the guests, the guns, the film, the money, the radios in the cars, the getaway. Concentrate and go over and over every detail of your plan.

The sun was up full over the Rhone valley as Saumur pulled off the main road into a deeply wooded area. We got out and stretched and set about preparing breakfast.

I could speculate now on how they had tipped to my trail. But speculation got me nowhere. Since I arrived in France, they had been, seemingly, one jump ahead of me. Every fear crowded my reason and demanded I call the mission off.

If they weren't waiting for me at the villa, it would be along the road somewhere. They knew everything else apparently, so why wouldn't they know about that.

Another question, without an answer.

21

The big Mediterranean moon hung above the Ruden villa like a giant Chinese lantern, creating furry shadows in the gardens below us. From our position, on the hill overlooking the villa we noted the arrival of each car carefully, counting the number of people who entered the garden and whether the car had a chauffeur, a footman, or both. Saumur had gone to hide our car two miles away.

I glanced at my watch. Five of ten. Not quite time to contact Otto yet.

"Three got out of that last one," Tookie reported softly to Gino. He lowered the binoculars. "One woman, two men."

"Chauffeur?" asked Gino, marking down the count.

"Just one," replied Tookie, and studied the house again.

"What's the count?" I asked Gino.

"Thirty-eight men, forty-seven women."

"There'll be more than that. Twice that many at least."

"Ten chauffeurs and two footmen. Most of them are driving their own cars," Gino said.

"Jesus," Tookie whispered. "A maharaja and four flunkies in the sweetest looking Rolls I ever saw!"

"Those are bodyguards," Gino said. "Check what they are wearing so we can check them out later."

"The big guy's in white—the others are in red," Tookie replied, eyes on the gate, looking through the binoculars.

"That car will be bulletproof, if I know my maharajas," Gino said. "I suggest we use that one to get away from the villa in."

"Okay," I said. "Check where it's parked."

Tookie followed the car with the glasses as it drove away from the main gate. There was a rustle of grass behind us and a moment later Saumur snaked into the clearing "Lower your guns, my friends."

"Ten o'clock," Gino said.

I nodded and picked up the walkie-talkie, pulled out the antenna and pressed the key. "Group one leader to group three—over."

"Group three." Otto's voice was soft.

"Everything all right?"

"Excellent. I have a complete coverage of the guards, gambling rooms and number of servants; and I think I can give you a pretty good word picture of the layout inside the walls."

"Go ahead," I said.

In clipped, concise sentences, Otto relayed the information to me over the talkie. Gino dotted down the details as I spoke them back to Otto.

There were ten guards, as near as he could figure out. Most of them inside the villa itself, probably on the gambling floor, which I could see from our position was the second. Two of the guards were at the front gate, two on the river side, while the terraced gardens were patrolled by two others. There were four cooks who remained in the kitchen, with ten waiters serving cocktails and attending the buffet where the supper was to be served. We had watched them setting up the tables since we arrived on the hill. Otto proposed waiting until the buffet was over and getting as many as possible on the second-floor gambling rooms.

I agreed with him. Getting as many of them together as possible was a question of watching the garden activity below. When the ranks thinned out, and before the early leavers started for their cars, would be the best time to move in.

Otto said it would not be difficult to take care of the three boat attendants on the dock and the two guards on the riverside terrace. I told Otto to go ahead and take care of the attendants and under no circumstances was he to use a gun. If he were caught, I assured him, we would do everything in our power to get him out.

Otto chuckled softly and said he would not get caught. We continued the car count below us, and I watched the motor pool on the side of our hill grow dark with automobiles. In the villa garden the mass of people were milling around the tables and it was not too difficult to single out the guards by their stiff posture and slow deliberate movements around the buffet tables. Music from two orchestras filtered up to us; the laughter and the tinkle of glasses caressed the hot humid night and complemented the music. For a half hour after midnight there had been no new arrivals. I glanced at my watch. Exactly twelve-thirty. Otto should have taken care of the dock attendants by now.

"Group three leader to group one."

"Boss, boss," Gino said softly beside me. "Otto's calling you."

I shook myself and grabbed the talkie. "Go ahead, group three."

"Success. All three of them are secure. We are ready down here."

"Prepare yourselves to move out."

"Very well."

I turned to Tookie. "Ready?"

"All set."

"Berets and masks," I said. We slipped the berets on and pulled them low over the black paint we had applied on our faces earlier. We tied the masks and slipped on the thin gloves; Tookie carried the nylon rope ladder slung in even coils over his shoulder. I slung the talkie over my shoulder and picked up the Thompson, slipping it over the opposite shoulder. Gino carried the other machine gun.

I called Otto on the talkie. "Synchronize watches— on the mark it will be exactly ten minutes past one." I watched the second hand climb around to the top of the clock face. "Mark!" I said.

"Check!" Otto replied.

"How much time do you need to take care of the guard on the terrace?" I asked Otto.

"Fifteen minutes."

"Very well. Tookie and I will move out toward the river side of the house at one-twenty-five. Watch for us—and cover our approach, which will be from your right facing the hilltop."

"Check."

"Take off," I said. The talkie went dead.

I turned to Gino and Saumur. "We should make the roof in fifteen minutes. That makes it one-forty. You have one hour—until two-forty—to take care of the cars and the chauffeurs, and hit the main gate guards."

"One hour. We have to be finished by two-forty," repeated Gino, nodding. He turned to Saumur. "That enough time?"

"Enough," said Saumur.

"At two-forty, on my signal, you move in on the front gate, Otto will move in from the rear—Tookie and I will come from the inside."

"Right," Gino said.

"Check your guns and gear," I said, breathing tightly. We checked over the guns, the spare clips and talkie sets, the face masks, shoelaces and gloves. The laughter from the villa grew louder. The music seemed more insistent. There were only a few guests left in the gardens now. And the guards were seen drinking wine. That helped.

"One-twenty-five," Tookie said beside me.

"Good luck!" I said to Gino and Saumur. "Wait for my call—wait three minutes—two-forty-three. If I don't call—we've been caught—and you come in after us."

Saumur nodded. "One hour," Gino said. "Good luck, boss."

Tookie and I moved out of the clearing of trees and made our way swiftly down the side of the hill, skirting the chauffeurs and the parked cars. Bending low, running on half-bent legs, we moved like shadows in the darkness.

We circled the cars and the villa and came up on the right side with a broad view of the river. There were no guards in sight. And while we watched, the dock lights went out. Two minutes later, the whole rear terrace was plunged into darkness.

"Let's go!" I said to Tookie.

We jumped up and ran full height through the gardens to the side of the villa. Tookie had the rope uncoiled and divided in his hands the moment we stopped.

"Make it good," I whispered to him.

He stepped back ten feet from the side of the villa, exposing himself in the light from the gambling rooms on the second floor and sent the hook singing around his head for momentum—and let fly.

For what seemed an eternity there was silence and only the whispering of the nylon cord uncoiling at Tookie's feet, then a distant *thump!* Tookie swung his weight on it.

It held.

He ran to the side of the building and darkness again, and without a word, began scrambling up the thin ladder. As soon as he cleared my head, I started climbing after him. The added weight of my body tightened the ladder and made it easy to climb.

On the roof, we hauled the line to the top. Incredibly Tookie had heaved the grappler into the chimney which we saw was the only place it could have gotten a hold on the pantile roof. Tookie hauled the ladder up quickly.

Crouching low, I called Otto. "Group one leader to group three, come in."

"Group three—we watched you go up. Everything is ready with us."

"Stay where you are. We must give group two time

to carry out their first phase. At exactly two-forty, I will contact you again."

"Yes." The talkie was silent.

I looked at my watch. One-forty-five; fifty-five minutes before Gino and Saumur would be finished.

"Do we sit and wait?" asked Tookie at my side.

"Search the roof for a trap door," I said, moving to my left and motioning him to his right.

We spent ten minutes wandering carefully across the top of the villa. In the far corner, overlooking the garden, we found what we were looking for. It was locked from the inside, but with the flat steel jimmy tools, we pried it open. The door came up and Tookie slipped inside instantly, dangling his feet into the dark hole and disappeared into the darkness. I slipped in after him, found the ladder and lowered the trap.

My flash revealed a bare storage room with a few trunks, dressmaking dummies and silken dust a half-inch thick covering forgotten oil paintings. The music and the laughter from inside the house was more distinct and personal now.

We found a door and opened it carefully. Steps in a dimly lighted stairway led down to a second door. We went down carefully.

"What's the idea of coming in so soon?" whispered Tookie.

"If we can search the top floor beforehand, we save time," I replied. "Open the door."

I unscrewed the bulb overhead. Tookie eased the door open onto a long, wide hall separating bedrooms. The music and the noise of the gambling rooms hit us solidly now. We could hear the croupier's call and the light click of dice and wheels.

"Start at the far end," I said motioning to the last

room.

Tookie nodded and padded down the hall before me, grotesque in the one-suit coveralls, sneakers, black beret, black face and mask. The talkie slung over one shoulder, the forty-five in his right hand. A mirror of my own self.

We slipped up to the door and listened. The rhythmic sounds and murmurings we heard were unmistakable.

Tookie grinned. "This oughta be easy."

"Ready?"

He nodded and opened the door. We went in together. The familiar sounds stopped immediately.

22

They were both nude, both drunk. The woman started to scream but Tookie slapped it out of her. The man sat on the side of the bed and stared at us, his mouth open, breathing hard, unable to move. We had them tied, mouths taped, and were out of the door in less than a minute.

We searched seven bedrooms and adjoining baths, and found another couple in the last room near the stairs. I recognized the woman. I had seen her face on the screen a dozen times. We tied them like the others and left the room, taking up a position behind the banister of the stairs.

"Watch it," Tookie hissed.

Three men were coming up the stairs abreast of each other. All of them were drunk. "They're queens!" Tookie said.

I motioned to let them pass us and come up from behind. He nodded. They came up quietly. The one in the middle couldn't have been more than eighteen—the other two were closer to forty. We let them pass and get halfway down the hall before we came up in back of them. Tookie chopped one down cleanly with a gun barrel on the neck, while I snapped the kid around, getting him in the stomach. The third, turning horrified, began clawing at Tookie's face. Tookie made a funny sound in his throat and brought his knee up sharply. The hands dropped and the thin body sagged to the floor.

We dragged them into the nearest bedroom and tied them like the two couples. "Outside," I whispered.

Tookie moved to the door and watched the hall. I pressed the talkie button. "Group three leader to group two—come in." Silence.

I called again. Silence. I looked at my watch. Fifteen minutes to go yet. I returned to the hall and took up a position across from Tookie. No one else came up the stairs.

At exactly two-forty, I pressed the button on the talkie and called Gino again.

"Group two leader. All clear here. Shall we move in on the gate?"

"Many left in the gardens?"

"About ten—most of them servants. The gate guards are a little drunk." Gino answered.

"Check in, group three," I said.

"Group three," Otto's voice replied.

"All set?"

"Ready."

I glanced at my watch. "In three minutes, group two moves on the garden—another minute and group three moves up from the terrace through the rear. Everyone comes to the gambling rooms."

"Check!" Gino said.

"Four minutes," Otto replied.

"Here we go!" I said into the talkie and released the button. I glanced at Tookie and nodded. He straightened up, the forty-five up. I slung the Thompson around with the strap across my shoulder so I could hold it with one hand, the forty-five in the other. "You go right as we enter and get to the other side of the room fast," I whispered. "If there's any shooting or resistance, shoot back, but get on the other side of the room and hold the door. Get 'em between us!"

"Check, sweetheart. And good luck."

"Move out," I said quietly, my heart pounding. I took the first step down, exposing myself to the milling throngs below. And with that first step, my fears, the danger, the indecision and doubt left me and I was cold and sure of myself.

We were nearly at the bottom of the stairs before we were spotted. A young girl turned away from conversation with a group and stared at us. She opened her mouth to scream, but nothing happened.

Tookie was halfway across the huge double room before anyone knew what was going on. A dozen people loitered in the stair chamber and from their comments, were not sure whether we were part of the evening's entertainment or the genuine article. I pulled up the Thompson and waved it at them. "Back inside," I called out.

Suddenly there was shooting outside. Several quick shots from a forty-five—then the quick chatter of Gino's Thompson.

The group before me who had hesitated understood. They tumbled backward—and then suddenly all hell broke loose. Next to me a guard went for his gun. I shot him with the forty-five and waved the Thompson again. The guard dropped to the floor holding his stomach.

"Back!" I roared. "Get back, or I open fire!" I waved the Thompson at them again.

Men and women fell back toward the opposite door in panic. Most of them had not seen Tookie glide through the room. There was a quick exchange of gunfire from Tookie's end of the room. And then the women began to really scream.

There was more gunfire from downstairs. Screams and running feet filtered up to me through the noise in the gambling rooms. The noise and shooting stopped momentarily and then came the authoritative voice of Gino's Thompson opening up in a long blast.

I moved so I could hold the stairs and the big rooms under cover and yelled over to Tookie. "Everything all right?"

"Check!"

Then I realized I had a talkie on my shoulder. I grinned. That helped me a lot. I pressed the key. "What was that shooting?" I asked Tookie.

"Stupid bastard tried to gun me … one of the maharaja's men."

The people were strangely silent, staring at me with wild-eyed, open fascination. "This is a holdup," I announced loudly. "If there is any resistance, I open fire with this." I held up the Thompson. "The villa is surrounded, telephones cut, and the guards, chauffeurs and servants taken care of."

A tall, immaculately dressed man with a withered left arm and three tiers of ribbons on his left breast strode toward me. "You wouldn't dare shoot—" his voice cracked with the insolence of an army officer used to command. I shot him in the good shoulder and swung back to the others.

"Another stupid mistake like that—" I let it hang there and waved the machine gun at them again.

"Line up!" I heard Tookie bawl from the other side of the room. "Men to the right, women to the left. Move!"

"Group two leader to group one." Gino's voice was calm.

"Go ahead."

"We got everybody locked up in a room downstairs, boss. I can hold them and send the other three up to help you. No need to herd them upstairs."

"Okay," I said.

I heard footsteps on the stairs almost immediately and a few seconds later Saumur, Marcus and Otto raced into view. They saw the docile, glittering group before me and grinned.

"Check your guns and reload," I said. "Anybody killed downstairs?"

"Saumur plugged one servant who got frisky," replied Otto with a grin. "But I don't think he's hurt badly."

"Gino fired the chopper in the air," Marcus said.

"Let's go to work," I said when they had finished reloading.

Otto, Marcus and Saumur advanced into the room where the men, women, servants and croupiers had lined the wall, hands behind their backs. Tookie stood opposite, his gun up and ready. He waved at us and grinned. The robed figure of the maharaja's guard lay sprawled nearby, moaning. Tookie reached over and picked up his gun and shoved it in his pocket.

In the center of the room—short, stocky, white-haired, his fleshy face blanched white as his stiff shirt front—

a man stared at me.

"Get in line!" Otto snarled.

"Take your hands off me, you scum!" the man said bitterly in French with the lisping accent of Spanish. "I am José Ruden—and if I have to spend the rest of my life apprehending you filth—"

Otto hesitated, then slapped him viciously across the face and shoved him toward the wall.

With Tookie at one end and myself at the other, Marcus, Saumur and Otto began stripping the tables of the money. Thick wads of currency were shoved into their coverall fronts. A large part of it was the harsh green of American dollars.

Ruden would not face the wall. He continued to watch us with something other than hate in his eyes. He stared at me hard.

"Get the jewels and wallets!" I ordered Otto, Saumur and Marcus.

A tremor of fear rippled through the women. The three started methodically searching the men and women. One beautiful young girl with burning eyes turned suddenly and ripped her rings off, thrusting them down the front of her dress and looked at Saumur defiantly. The big Frenchman reached out and caught the top of her gown and ripped it to the waist exposing her flat, hard little belly and breasts. The rings clattered to the floor. Saumur reached to pick them up and the woman seized this moment to try and rake his face. Saumur anticipated her movement and slapped her so hard she bounced off the wall and slid to the floor.

Ruden had not taken his eyes off me. I watched him. I picked up the talkie and pressed the key. "Everything okay group two?"

"Check! How's with you?" replied Gino.

"Fine. Be finished up here in a few minutes."

I released the key and called Tookie over. "Take this." I slipped the Thompson off my shoulder and handed it over to him.

"What's up?"

"I'll show you." I nodded toward Ruden and walked toward him. "The safe, M'sieu!" I announced loudly for everyone to hear. "If you please?"

He stared at me. His mouth twitched. "In the study," he said. He nodded toward the opposite door.

I walked him across the room and opened the door, the forty-five in his back. The room was high-ceilinged and circular bookshelves covered the walls. He went to a shelf nearest the bay window and removed several books revealing the safe.

"Open it," I said.

He turned and glanced over his shoulder, looking at the door to the gambling room. "Are you a friend of Von Walter?" he asked softly.

"Open it," I said.

He opened the safe and stepped aside. I rifled it, tearing letters and documents open looking for the film. But it wasn't there. A ring with a diamond the size of my thumb lay by itself on the bottom of the safe. I picked it up and dropped it in my pocket.

"Von Walter?" he asked again.

"Strip!" I barked.

He began taking off his clothes without another word handing each piece to me. I searched the seams carefully. There was nothing. Not even in the buckled slippers he wore, which twisted apart easily in my hands.

"Teeth!" I said.

That was it. His eyes faded and then focused on me hard and bright. He slipped the double dentures out of his mouth, his face sinking in, making him look twenty years older. I cracked them with my gun butt. Three back molars shattered in my hands revealing a pencil-thick twist of dark film. I unrolled the first frame while he watched me and held it up to the light of the gambling room.

Across the top of the blueprint were the words HOCH GEHEIMNIS and the signature of FRITZ HEMER beneath it. And on the bottom of the frame, a circular stamp or seal.

I think I must have stopped breathing at that moment. I twisted the film back up and dropped it into my pocket. "Tell them I want a million pounds," he said to me. "I will not take less than a million pounds. Von Walter promised me—"

"I don't know what you're talking about," I said harshly.

He grabbed my arm. "A million pounds! I must have it!"

Saumur stood just inside the door watching us. "*Sacré bleu!* You *are* intelligence!"

I turned and stared at him dumfounded. Then he suddenly brought up his gun, shouted something and fired. Ruden screamed behind me.

I dropped to the floor and fired on the way down, snapping it at him and feeling the heavy gun buck against my elbow. "You don't understand," he gasped and sprawled back on the floor.

I was confused. I turned and looked at Ruden. Saumur had saved my life. Ruden still held a short ornate pistol gripped tightly in his right hand. I had not seen it and if Saumur had not entered at that moment, he would have slipped it in my stomach. Saumur's shot had drilled him neatly in the heart. I staggered to Saumur's side and dropped to the floor.

He fluttered his eyelids. He coughed and spit on the floor. He closed his eyes and opened them again. A smile touched his lips. "*Carte du pays*, M'sieu. You planned too carefully—you were too good a criminal to be a criminal, but I could not be sure you were intelligence," he grinned. "This was the first time—I was sure—"

"And you're French intelligence?" I said. "Why didn't you let me know some way?"

"*Ruse de guerre*, boss," he said with difficulty. "I could not risk ..." He lifted a finger and pointed toward Ruden. "Did the little one give you the film?"

"Yes—I have it—" My mind was racing. "One of the others is a Red," I said. "Do you know which one it is?"

He coughed again—and died.

Tookie rushed into the room "What happened?"

"He started shooting," I indicated Ruden, "and got Saumur."

"Tough," Tookie said flatly, and began stripping the loot from Saumur's coveralls, stuffing them into his own.

Otto appeared. He glanced around and saw the dead Ruden. His eyes clouded over. "What happened to him?"

"He was holding out on me. I made him strip to make sure and got this for my efforts." I held up the heavy diamond ring. "Let's get out of here!"

"What about Saumur?" asked Tookie.

"He has no identification," I said. "And it'll be at least twenty-four hours before they can check his fingerprints. Leave him."

"He would have made a wonderful ranch partner,"

Otto said almost gently.

I pressed the button on the talkie. "Come in Gino—we're finished upstairs."

"All clear."

"Let's go," I said to them.

Marcus remained on guard in the doorway of the stair chamber and the gambling room. The women were turning now to stare at us.

We raced down the stairs to the main floor. The upstairs rooms erupted into screams of hysteria as the guests realized we were gone. The garden was a mess of overturned tables. A man lay on the ground. Evidence of Gino's machine gun was everywhere. We ran out of the gate with Gino in the lead, Tookie covering our rear.

We found the sleek Rolls and Tookie slipped under the wheel. In seconds he sent the car slashing through the darkness, past the villa where we heard shouts, curses and screams. But all that faded in a moment and we were alone in the car.

No one said a word. Every man was busy reloading his weapons and when that was finished, lighting cigarettes. I pulled out a flask of brandy and each of us took a heavy drink.

Five minutes after we had left the villa, we had changed over to our own car and driven the Rolls into the Rhone River. Twelve minutes after our retreat, we were on the outskirts of St. Giles.

The wind began to pick up, blowing dust across the roads—a heavy hard wind out of the southeast that could be the beginning of a storm.

23

It is roughly eighty miles from Arles to Beziers. We covered the distance in less than fifty minutes. By the time we stopped for the twenty-five-gallon can of gasoline Saumur I had stored away, we had removed the black makeup, the coveralls and sneakers. While Marcus and Otto filled the tank, Gino, Tookie and I beat our way deep into the dense brush on the side of the road and dug a hole. We buried everything we had used in the raid except the guns, ammo and large battery set, fighting the increasing wind as we did.

We were back on the road in nine minutes with the radio tuned to police frequencies. Tookie continued to drive, with Marcus helping him with directions from the maps and keeping a lookout for danger.

Otto crouched on the floor of the back, with Gino and myself on either side of the huge mound of currency before us. We began counting and stacking the dollars, francs and pounds in bundles of ten thousand dollars each. The jewelry was collected and wrapped in a handkerchief and put to one side for later.

On the outskirts of Narbonne, twenty-five miles further than Beziers, we got the first flash of the raid over the radio. We stopped and listened carefully. The alert was for a dozen men, probably traveling in two or more cars. There was no description of the cars or the men except that officials were to shoot to kill on sight. Two had been killed at the villa and four wounded. The alert was repeated over and over, but no new information came across, except that we had probably made our initial getaway in a 1950 four-door Rolls Royce.

We moved through the quiet sleepy streets of Narbonne without incident. We saw no one at all on the sidewalks. Once outside, Tookie pressed his foot to the floor again and we raced on through the darkness, continuing to count the fantastic amount of money on the back seat.

"What happens to Saumur's cut?" asked Tookie.

"Split it four ways," I said. "All I want is one-half off the top."

"That sounds fair," said Otto.

"Agreed," Gino said. Tookie nodded.

We continued counting until we reached the edge of Perpignan, where I told Tookie to pull over to the side of the road. "Gino will look out for your cut, Marcus," I said. "Get out and keep guard. This is the split."

He moved out the door and disappeared in the darkness "What's the count?" I asked Gino.

He looked at me, his eyes wide, sweat running down the side of his face "Seven hundred and twenty-four grand, four hundred and change." He licked his lips. "Nearly two hundred G's in American, three hundred in pounds and the rest francs."

"We call it seven twenty in round figures," I said. "I get half the pounds, dollars and francs. And I deduct ten grand for my investment." I looked at them. "Any complaints?"

They were silent. I reached over to the money and pulled the stacks toward me. "I'll take a hundred grand in dollars, a hundred and fifty in pounds and ninety-five in francs—with my ten for expenses that comes to three-seven-o," I said.

"Three-seven-o," Tookie said, his voice level, flat and

without emotion. "Now get outa here and I split up the rest."

I shoved my money into one of the small bags we had brought along and got out of the car.

"What's the count?" asked Marcus softly in back of me.

I told him. "I'll take the guard," I said.

"*Mama mia*," he whispered. He slid into the car, shoving the Thompson in my hands. I walked down the road a hundred feet and looked around. The wind was definitely coming directly out of the southeast Mediterranean Sea and was blowing wild now.

I climbed a small rise on the side of the road and slipped the film out of my pocket, kicking off my right shoe. I removed the inner sole over the heel. Wrapping the film carefully in several American five-hundred-dollar bills, I slipped it back inside and retied the shoe.

A piece of film. What did it cost? In money, lives, effort, all that could be estimated and a value set on it. But what about the cost to me? As a man? Eh? What about that, M'sieu?

And the end not in sight.

"All set boss," Tookie said below me.

We went back to the car and started off again.

24

There was nothing new on the radio. They still thought we were using the Rolls to make our get away. The estimate on our number had dropped to eight. There was, as yet, no identification of the one member of the gang that had been killed.

Had Saumur known who the Judas was? I was too

tired to go back over the twisting trails of a look, a gesture, an inflection of speech to decide if Saumur had known. Certainly in the long hours we had been together, he had played his role expertly. Of course, from the perspective of knowing the end, I could look back and see how the fight at the Inn de Mosel outside of Arles that night had been staged.

I was too tired. I could not think about it anymore. Only that I had the film and that I was still keeping company with a man who would wait until the right moment to try and take it from me.

It was getting lighter as we approached the outskirts of Elne. Tookie drove through the slowly awakening streets without incident. It was getting lighter, but it would still be another half hour before the good hard light of dawn.

A flash of lightning cracked across the sky, followed by a distant roll of thunder. And almost at once, unannounced, strong gusts of wind scooped up sand from the side of the road, blasting the car.

It began to rain. Slowly at first. The big heavy drops of water splashing on the windshield.

We were under twenty miles from the Spanish border when the storm broke powerfully out of the Gulfe du Lion and threw itself violently onto the Roussillon-Languedoc coasts. "More speed," I said to Tookie. "We can take advantage of the rain."

"Hang on," he said quietly.

We raced through the country, slipping and sliding on the dangerous roads. We found the outskirts of Port Vendres, where we would pick up the guide, covered with water. And into the small community itself, the flooding waters from the rains poured over the gutters and onto the sidewalks.

I directed Tookie down the street to the spot where we were supposed to pick up the guide.

The corner was empty. "Park," I said. "We'll wait few minutes."

Tookie pulled over to the side of the street and stopped. He kept the motor running. He lit a cigarette. Marcus, Otto and Gino sat in the back of the car, their faces wooden as they scanned the streets and buildings for some sign of our guide.

"How much longer?" asked Tookie without looking at me. He touched the accelerator gently, racing the motor.

"Give him another few minutes," I said.

"I wanta move," Tookie said flatly.

"Check!" Gino said in back of me.

"We can't afford to wait," Otto said levelly.

I sat still. I studied the streets outside the car; the graying-over rainswept streets. "Okay, take off."

Tookie had the car in gear before I finished speaking. I directed him out of town toward the border road.

"This is the last stretch?" asked Tookie. "What do we do, crash the station?"

I was silent. There was one way to find out which was the Judas and damned quick. If we split up, either one of them would play his hand or I would get away.

I gripped the forty-five in my pocket and dropped my hand on the Thompson. I took a deep breath. I opened my mouth to speak.

I spoke. "Pull—"

"Boss! Boss!" Marcus screamed in my ears. "We're being followed!"

"Sûreté!" breathed Gino. "But how—"

"I'll lose'm," said Tookie and jammed his foot onto the floor. The car leaped ahead into the storm. The rear window suddenly disintegrated and a bullet ringed over our heads, burying itself into metal and upholstery.

"Down!" I yelled.

Another bullet—and then another—followed by many more. Tookie began to weave the car, whipping it heavily from side to side. "Get 'em!" I snapped. I didn't care who was back there. They were trying to kill me.

Gino brought the Thompson up and shoved it through he shattered window. I ducked low in the seat. Gino began firing at once.

Tookie drove with tense anticipation. He screamed at me, "Do we crash the station?"

"Slow down!" I answered. "Keep those guns going!" Otto and Marcus had joined in the shooting.

"We got the front car!" Gino yelled. He pulled back to reload and I handed over the Thompson sitting on my lap. Otto and Marcus continued taking pot shots at the other cars. "There's three of them!" Gino yelled as he went back to work with the Thompson.

"How far have we come from Port-Vendres?" I yelled at Tookie.

"Five—six miles," he answered as I reloaded the machine gun.

I stuck my head up and glanced around at the road. The countryside was getting progressively jagged and more rugged as we climbed the lower hills of the Pyrenees. The cars hung on our tail.

"Pull over at the next blind turn. Everybody out and into the rocks. If we crash the border station, they'll nail us in Spain. Our only chance is to get lost in the hills!"

The cars had dropped back a good thousand yards

now, when Tookie yelled. "Here's the curve—and good rocks to climb into!"

He spun the car around the curve with careless control and slammed on the brakes. Otto and I were on the ground a moment after he put his foot on the brake. "Don't cut the engine," I warned.

Otto, Gino and Marcus had already started climbing into the rocks. "Turn the car around and get it back around the curve!"

Understanding flashed across his face at once. I grabbed the Thompson and stepped out into the road and opened fire on the two approaching cars. Tookie had twisted the car around and headed back down the road straight for the two approaching cars. He jumped and ran to my side.

Our car careened crazily down the road. The two cars stopped, skidding to one side trying to avoid the speeding car, but there was no room. Our car smashed into the first one and spun it around, turning it over directly into the second.

A gas tank exploded. A man screamed.

We stood in the middle of the road, guns ready, watching the fire turn into smoke, waiting for signs of life. Nothing in either of the two cars moved. The storm slashed around us. I motioned Tookie forward and approached the cars cautiously. If there were anyone alive in the cars, and if they were who I thought they were, then it would be necessary—I blocked the thought out and approached the first car. Three men were inside, burned, dead. They wore the black suit, the anonymous black suit, like the four in the Lyon woods. We checked the second car. One man was alive, groaning and in shock. Three others in the car were dressed like the rest.

I tried to ease it a little by thinking he wouldn't live anyway and shot him through the head.

"How did they spring to our tail?" Tookie asked. He shook his head in amazement. "I tell ya, they crawl outa the woodwork!" He picked up a fire-scorched Luger. "Did you get what you were after back at the villa?" he asked suddenly, examining the Luger and dropping it back into the smoking car.

"No," I lied.

He looked at me, his rain-wet face hard and tight. "You wouldn't have left the goddamn villa until you had," he said harshly. He turned on his heel and started climbing into the rocks.

I turned back to the cars. The fire had stopped completely now. And the smoke dissipated before it rose ten feet.

I stared into the thick rain. Up ahead of me, rising high and disappearing in the clouds and the rain, were the Pyrenees, and the Spanish border was—how many miles away? I stuffed the bag of currency into my shirt and scrambled into the rocks after the others.

Suddenly I stopped. I looked up over me at the others. Why take a chance and go on with them? I had the film and it would be simple to operate alone. Then I remembered I had to go on. The letter from Boyler with instructions ... "They must believe, though they do not have the film, that it is unobtainable and in fact has vanished from the face of the earth...."

Gino? Marcus? Otto? Tookie? Which one had to die to put an end to Operation Sentinel? I was still betting on Tookie.

25

We found a four-foot-wide donkey track about nine-thirty, and by eleven, when the storm seemed to be reaching its peak, we had followed it without stopping. It was difficult to see more than a few hundred yards ahead of us. The winds whistled and drove the rain into our eyes and faces with stinging ferocity. I do not know how many times I fell to the ground and pulled myself back up, only to be staggered by the wind. Heavy black clouds raced out of the sea and seemed close enough to touch.

Twelve noon and the sky was black. There was no way of telling whether we had crossed the border. The rocks rose around us and before us in an impossible barrier. Countless times we passed along the trail beside drops of more than a hundred feet, and after that, the rain closed in and left the imagination to dwell on what lurked below the impenetrable mists.

I was leading, dragging the sodden, weighty bag of currency along in the muddy trail, stumbling blindly. Tookie was being held up by Gino, with Otto and Marcus straggling a hundred yards behind.

I turned a corner in the trail and found a shallow depression carved out of the rocky wall, just deep enough to protect us from the rain and wind if we stood with our backs jammed up against the inner side. I stopped and, one by one, they joined me. Gino and Marcus stood to the side and spoke softly to each other in Italian. Otto remained erect, keeping to himself, staring back down the trail. Tookie was completely exhausted and coughed constantly.

"I gotta get outa this," he said to no one in particular. "If I don't, I'll die right here in these lousy goddamn mountains."

I glanced at my watch. Quarter to one. We had been climbing steadily since before six that morning. The storm was perfect cover for our climbing and the escape, but I was looking forward to the night. We had to have shelter. I stepped to the edge of the depression and stared up the trail. "I'll go ahead," I said, "and see if I can find something or someone that can get us out of this."

Tookie looked up at me. "You wanta split up?"

Otto turned and stared silently, his blue eyes distant and thoughtful. Gino and Marcus looked from Tookie to me.

"I think it's best," Tookie said in a measured way, "that we stick together. Until we hit a big town."

"We need shelter," I said. "What happens if this thing keeps going all night? The temperature drops near freezing in these mountains at night—and we're soaking wet, with nothing to burn."

"We can't risk a fire," Gino said hastily.

So Tookie didn't want to split up, I thought. That's reasonable, if he believes I've got the film. And he believes it. "You've got your share of the loot," I said harshly. "There wasn't anything in the agreement that said we have to stick together."

I turned up the trail, speaking to them over my shoulder. "I'll see what's up ahead."

I moved on up the rocky slopes about two hundred yards and stepped behind a boulder and waited. Someone would follow me, if he wanted that film.

There was a movement further down. I pulled the Thompson up and held it steady. The rain slackened for a moment.

It was Tookie—and on either side of him, Otto and Gino holding him under the arms. "Why break up a winning combination?" he growled as he passed me. "What're you waiting on, a streetcar?"

Marcus drew up alongside of me and grinned. "Wet, eh?"

I watched them stagger on up the trail and disappear into the rain and mists.

Would he make his move along the trail? Where a push could be explained away as a slip?

No, there wouldn't be any way to get the film if it were done that way. And he would have to kill me to get the film.

It would come later, after we had gotten out of the mountains, and there would be the cover of a city to escape into.

Not in the mountains, but as soon as we were free of them, I thought, moving after them up the narrow donkey track.

26

The trail dropped sharply and we stood facing the desolate muddy street of a village. There were nine cottages smaller buildings and a church.

An organ began playing the Wedding March.

"I'll be a bat-faced bastard!" Tookie wheezed.

Otto had moved to the top of a rock and watched the village carefully. "No one moving around," he said, climbing back down.

"In a village this size, if there is a wedding going on," Gino said, "it's ten to one everybody is in the church."

"We'll make sure," I said. "Gino, you and Marcus search the cottages for dry clothes and food and bring anyone you find to the church. Tookie, Otto and myself will be waiting for you."

The two brothers slipped out and moved toward the first cottage, while the rest of us approached the church. We checked the gardens and then moved to the windows. About thirty-five adults and twenty-odd children watched a laced and robed priest celebrate before a kneeling bride and groom. Step by step we watched the solemn office continue through to its end. When it was over, the couple stood up and faced the church. An old woman rushed to the girl and began to cry as she embraced her. A few men got up and came forward hesitantly to shake hands with the groom. Others moved forward until their enthusiasm began to get the better of them, and singing, the whole congregation surrounded the happy couple and began pressing them toward the back door.

Otto quickly circled to enter from the rear while Tookie and I stormed the front I waved the Thompson. "Remain where you are!"

Women began to scream and several men dashed toward the rear of the church only to meet Otto coming in. The church settled back in dumfounded silence.

The priest swept past the wedding couple, eyes burning fire. "You dare desecrate the House of God!"

"Shut up!" growled Otto.

"Ruffians!" hissed the priest. "I am not afraid of you! Get out. Get out!"

Otto moved to grab the priest but Tookie was between them, shoving the German back. "You touch him and they'll tear you apart. Ya dumb kraut-head."

I moved past them and grabbed the bride by the

wrist and turned to the villagers staring at me in sullen, defiant silence. The groom pushed around his new wife and made for me, but Tookie shoved him to one side. "Get back!" he growled. For the first time I noticed the differences in the wedding couple's age. He must have been near fifty, while she was a girl of twenty, if that.

"We do not want to harm any of you," I said in a loud voice. "We must stay here until the storm is over."

The priest, who had remained at my side, pressed closer to me. "Release that child!"

She was looking at me. Blond hair pulled back tightly, she breathed quickly, her full breasts rising and falling, a curious bright look in her eyes. She turned very slowly, positively, and began speaking to her new husband in a cold voice. She spoke rapidly, now allowing the man to reply, in a jargon of half French and half Spanish at first, and then shifted over to French all together. "Are you going to do nothing?" she demanded.

The people in the church murmured among themselves. The groom was still, his face pale and he looked around at the villagers quickly. He spoke gently, but she did not listen.

"Is this what I have to look forward to when we live together?" she said, continuing in the cold, impersonal voice. "The memory of your cowardice on our wedding day? Isn't it enough that I marry you, M'sieu, to please my mother and father so they can be taken care of in their old age, and to marry a man old enough to be my father," she turned to face the villagers, speaking directly to them, but still addressing herself to her husband, "isn't it enough, M'sieu, without having the whole village, all my friends, know that you are a coward, as well as a miser, indulgent and selfish?" She took a deep breath. "Eh? Speak to me, now, M'sieu!"

"Be quiet, Sidony!" he said hoarsely, glancing around.

"Isn't it enough—" she started again, but he slapped her across the face. The villagers groaned and murmured. She took the blow and glared at him. "You struck the wrong one, M'sieu," she said gently, reprovingly.

"Shut up!"

"They are the criminals, not me," she said.

"Sidony—please!" a woman, who must have been her mother, pleaded.

"Be quiet, old lady!" she said.

"You speak to your mother that way," the priest said, turning to her, anger in his voice. He spun around on me. "This is the effect you have had on us!" he screamed shrilly. "You've turned this poor girl into a—"

"I am not poor any longer, Father," Sidony said, watching her husband closely. "I married a wealthy man. But I wonder if my children will be cowards— gutless, weak-livered men like him, eh, Father?"

"Sidony—my god! They have guns!" the man pleaded. "They are criminals—murderers!"

"Cowardly wretch!" She screamed for the first time.

"Coward—coward! I'll show you—I'll—" he bellowed. He spun away from Tookie and plowed through the mass of villagers crowding around us, roaring like a bull.

Sidony's expression was eager, her eyes bright and hard as she watched her husband run toward the door.

Otto stood before the door waiting for him. The man swung awkwardly and Otto dodged it easily, chopping the man down with his gun. The man got up and rushed in again. Brutally, with methodical efficiency, the German beat the man to the floor with his gun butt.

Sidony stood biting her lower lip, watching the two men, and now ran toward her husband, Tookie and I right behind her. Otto lounged against the wall and grinned at us.

"Ya did a pretty good job, kraut," Tookie said with an edge to his voice. "You had plenty of fun."

"Would you want him to escape?" Otto asked.

Sidony dropped down beside her husband and felt his heart. Eyes flashing, she leaned over and listened to his breathing.

She looked up, her mouth twisted into a grimace, his blood smeared on her cheek. "Why didn't you shoot? Why didn't you kill him and make me a widow?" she said to Otto.

The German looked at me.

"Wow!" Tookie said. "Wow and goddamn!"

27

About 4:00 A.M. the wind stopped, but the rain continued just as heavily. The priest and several of the women had worked over Sidony's husband, but he was still unconscious. Sidony had not gone near him. She sat alone, staring straight ahead. Most of the villagers were asleep. Gino and Marcus had returned with heavy sheepskin jackets for each of us and several bottles of wine and cheese. The two brothers were now on guard duty, Marcus in the bell tower and Gino on the back door. I sat on the altar smoking when Tookie walked over to me. He sat down beside me and lit a cigarette. "We've practically got it made now, boss," he said softly.

"Wanta tell me what this caper was *really* about?"

"Stay on your side of the fence, Tookie," I said. "Lay off."

"It ain't right a guy like me, giving you the support I have, should be left out in the cold."

"What do you want to know for? You got your loot. Isn't that enough?"

"Just curiosity," he said, grinning.

"It killed the cat."

"Won't kill me," he said.

"Lemme tell you something, Tookie. Just brushing with this thing might get you a slug in the head. From either side."

"Sure, I figure that. But if I know what's cooking, I can protect myself."

"In this case, Tookie, I would advise ignorance."

"I'm going to find out, boss. One way or the other, I'm going to find out."

"Not from me."

Tookie nodded his head that he would.

"You play a game with me, Tookie, and I'll put a slug in your head," I said softly.

His face grew tight. "I might blast you just to prove you're wrong."

"Start blasting," I said.

"Ahhhh, drop dead, ya limey bastard," he said exasperatedly, and moved away, stretching out on one of the pews and closing his eyes.

I moved to one of the windows and looked out into the dark night and listened to the rain beat a tattoo against the glass. There was movement at my side. I turned and looked down at Sidony.

"You are escaping criminals, is that not so, M'sieu?"

"You better go sit down. They've got it in for you as it

is. If they see you talking to me—" I shrugged.

"There is only one way out of this village," she said. "The way you came in."

"So?"

"But I know another way—a secret way. If you promise to take me with you, I will show it to you."

I watched her closely. "Anyone clever enough to goad your new husband into possible death trying to escape, leaving you a widow, might possibly lead us into a trap," I said.

Her eyes were desperate. "Do you have any idea what he will do to me when you leave?"

"I have an idea," I said. "And I can't say that I blame him."

She looked me in the eye. "He used to follow me into the mountains when I climbed after the flock—he boasted for years that he would marry me. He is the richest man in the village and naturally my mother and father—" she shrugged, dropping her eyes. "But that is not so bad." She took a deep breath and straightened her neck proudly. "One day, many years ago—I was fourteen or fifteen—it was hot in the mountains. I went for a swim—and he appeared. I begged him to go away—but he wouldn't. He stood there grinning, holding my clothes—watching me. His eyes—"

"Are you sure about this pass through the mountains?" I asked, cutting her off.

"M'sieu, I was born in these mountains. All my life I have chased the flock. There is a pass, M'sieu."

"Where do we come out—in Spain?"

"Near Figueras."

"How far from Figueras to Barcelona?"

She shrugged. "More than a hundred kilometers."

"What will you do when we get through the pass?"

"Perhaps I will go to Madrid, or Zaragoza. There are canneries there and I can get a job. My father took me there once as a little girl." She looked at me. "Perhaps you will give me a little money."

"You get us through the mountains into Spain safely and you won't have to work in a cannery," I said.

I got up and moved softly among the sleeping villagers to Tookie and Marcus. I signaled Gino and Otto to come over. I told them of Sidony's proposition. They agreed to it without hesitation.

Sidony nodded and walked to the door, slipping out. She didn't even look back. We followed her, closing the door softly behind us, and hurried down the village street.

Near the last cottage, Sidony turned in and signaled us to wait. She went inside and came out a few minutes later dressed in trousers and boots, carrying a sheepskin jacket. She handed Marcus a leather pouch with cheese and bread and turned into the darkness. "This way—hurry!" she whispered.

She moved off into the darkness. In back of us, the church was quiet.

28

The rain stopped about six and by ten the Pyrenees were baking in a dry heat. I don't know how high we were but it was enough to make Tookie cough continuously. The thin air put a strain on all of us except Sidony who hopped and leaped and climbed as sure-footedly as her goats. We had not stopped since leaving the village and more than once we had hesitated in following her through a dangerous trail, only to watch her uncover a simple way through. It was exactly high noon when we entered a small, boxed canyon and Sidony turned to face us. "We can stop for a rest now." She pointed to one of the sheer rock walls. "We will have to climb that."

"How much further?" I asked.

"To where?"

"Across the border."

"We crossed that about five hours ago. You are now in Spain." She walked away into a clump of wild cork oaks.

"Tookie looks better already," Gino said with a grin.

"Picking up this dame is luckier than marrying the boss' daughter and inheriting the store," Tookie said, without coughing.

The canyon, small and neat, was enveloped on three sides by straight walls of rock. The floor was a thick brush of coarse grass and curious lavender and white flowers. The ornamental cork oak trees dotted the ground, some of them stripped years before of their precious bark. Set into the side of the farthest wall of the canyon, a cave with an opening about twenty-five feet in diameter was cool and darkly inviting.

It was absolutely still.

Sidony returned from the trees and stood on the edge of our circle, biting her lip and staring at us.

"Thirsty, sweetheart?" Tookie passed along a bottle of wine.

She didn't move. Her eyes were bright. She bit her lips hard.

"How much more do we climb after we get outa here?" I asked.

She didn't answer.

"What's on the other side of the canyon?"

"It's all downhill after that," she said. She opened her mouth to say something else and then closed it tight. She seemed scared to death.

I jumped up beside her. "What is it?"

"You're going to kill me!" she said suddenly. "You—will think I betrayed you. But I didn't! I swear it!"

The others jumped up.

"What's going on?" I demanded.

"We're being followed," she said, fighting back the tears. "I saw them—he is leading them."

Otto grabbed her roughly. "Who is leading who?"

"Lay off that stuff, Otto," Gino said.

"My husband—they are just passing the big stream we crossed this morning."

"Is there any way we can get out of here without their seeing us?"

She turned and pointed toward the canyon wall, the one with the cave. "It will take four or five hours to get to the top—by that time they will be here—and see us."

"There's got to be another way," Tookie said.

She shook her head.

Otto said something in German and slapped her across the face. His hands began to shake, his face drawn white. Tookie stepped back and brought up the Thompson. "You do that again, kraut, and I'll chop you in half."

Sidony jerked free and stumbled away. "I swear I did not do this on purpose, M'sieu," she said to me. "No one knows this pass but me—"

"Then how did they follow us?" demanded Otto.

"Shut up," I said. "Use your head. We could have left a trail in the dark simple enough for a child to follow."

"Never mind the talk," Gino said nervously. "We gotta do something fast."

"We could take up positions and pick them off before they knew what hit them," suggested Tookie. "How many of them are there, sweetheart?"

"Fourteen—fifteen, counting my husband."

"Villagers?" Marcus asked.

She shook her head. "Not all of them. Many of them were strangers. They came to our village yesterday, and said they were waiting for friends to accompany them into Spain."

"Well, I'll be a sonofabitch," exploded Tookie, and turned to look at me, as did Otto, the German's eyes clouding over.

"What's with the crazy looks at each other?" demanded Gino.

They were Reds. There was no doubt about it. The possibility of their being Sûreté did not fit into the pattern of what had happened before. The four in the Lyon woods suddenly appearing, the three cars waiting for us in Port-Vendres, and now up here in the mountains. Like Tookie said, they seemed to crawl right out of the woodwork. Except that there was obviously little guesswork and more meticulous planning behind their ability to stay on our trail— even be ahead of it. I ignored Gino's question and turned to the canyon wall, my eyes hanging on the cave. "Can we get to that cave?"

"We might," Sidony said.

"What's inside?" Marcus asked.

"I have never been inside, M'sieu," Sidony replied.

"What'cha wanta hole up in a cave for?" asked Tookie. "They find you in there and then where you going to run?"

"If we're in the cave—we might be able to get out after dark," I said. "Can we do that?" I asked Sidony.

"Yes, you can climb after dark," Sidony replied. "It is dangerous, but it can be done."

Gino turned and stared at the rock face. "You mean try and climb that goddamn thing in the *dark?*"

"The alternative is to stand and fight—or ambush them. But they've got us outnumbered three to one, and if we do fight, we'll have the border patrol down on us in an hour when the shots start echoing in these mountains."

They all looked at me.

"Okay," I said. "I'm for trying to get up that wall— and if we can make it now, hide in the cave and wait for dark."

No one said anything. "But we'll take a vote on it."

"Marcus and I follow you," Gino said instantly, getting up and collecting his guns. "It's your play right down the line." He looked at the others.

"I'm for running," Tookie said, nodding his head in agreement.

Otto nodded his head curtly.

I turned to Sidony. "You get us over that wall and I promise we will make you a rich woman." I held up the handkerchief full of jewelry we had not yet divided and looked at the others. They nodded their heads as one in agreement.

"*Oui*, M'sieu, I will try," Sidony said. She turned and started running lightly across the floor of the canyon. One by one we trailed out after her.

29

The wall Sidony was going to climb was well over three hundred feet to the top, and except for a few ledges here and there, and the cave, seemed impossible to climb. "We'll try to make the cave first," I said. "Then if we have time—we'll try for the top from there."

Sidony nodded and stepped around the base of the wall and fifty or sixty feet from where we were standing, began working her way upward. Gino, Tookie, Otto, Marcus and I followed her.

Clinging to the face of the rock, working our way upward on two- and three-inch steps, clinging to ledges with fingertips, passing information down to the next fellow on exactly where to grab and where to place his foot, we made about seventy-five feet the first hour.

At one-thirty, the sun broke out from behind a mountain and began beating down on our backs. In a half hour the side of the wall was blistering hot. We could not turn back, we could not stop. We could only follow the next fellow's instructions as they were relayed down from the top from Sidony, and keep climbing.

Quarter past two and we had made 150 feet. Halfway, but with the roughest part yet to come. The sun had really begun to bear down now. The rock holds we touched were just short of unbearable. Another twenty feet and we stopped for a rest on a small rocky ledge and tasted the wine. There was no escaping from the sun. The canyon floor was green and hot. After a five-minute rest, we started out again.

We were still seventy-five feet short of the cave, which

we could see a little to our left. I don't think there was one of us that didn't appreciate what Sidony was doing. It was difficult to remember her as the pale blonde girl dressed so daintily, kneeling before the priest, being married. Even when she had inflamed her husband into trying to escape, she had still been a young woman. But now, the heavy boots and sheepskin coat swung on a loop around her neck and dangling down her back, moving surely from one desperate foothold to another, she was the epitome of a mountain girl who had lived her life among the craggy heights, tending her goats.

Gino, right below her, had been careful to relay information down to us on exactly what to grab for, or where to place our feet; he cursed suddenly. A trickle of gravel and pebbles tumbled down on us. "Watch out below!" he bellowed.

We hugged the wall, pressing our cheeks up against the baking rock to avoid the falling stones. The slide fell down on us. Otto cursed in German. Marcus, who was right above me, began to curse violently. He had gotten something in his eyes and could not see.

"Gino! Ginoooo!" he screamed.

"Shut up!" Gino yelled down to him.

"I can't see—I can't see what I'm doing—Ginooo!"

"Shut up!" Gino cursed him. "Open your eyes. Open them!"

"I can't—I can't," Marcus said pleadingly. "What am I going to do—Ginoooo!"

"Open them!" Gino commanded, his voice thundering in the silence of the canyon.

Marcus began to cry. There was no way for Otto to help him and it was impossible for him to return to the ledge below.

"Get a rope," Marcus pleaded, "get something—help me, Gino, my God, help me. I can't hold on much longer."

"Open your eyes, you yellow dog," Otto said harshly. "No one can help you but yourself."

"Open up!" Gino demanded.

"I can't—I can't—I'm slipping—"

I dared looking up at him. If he fell he would fall right on top of me. I took a step upward, moving within a few feet of his foothold and locked both arms around a jagged rock, hugging it with all my strength.

"Gino—I'm falling—"

"Marcussss!"

He fell. Sliding downward along the side of the wall, hitting me hard on the shoulder. I turned and watched him slipping, bouncing against the side of the wall straight down to the canyon floor.

He landed in a jackknife, his backbone snapping with the dry crack of an old piece of wood, and lay still.

Pebbles and more gravel began falling down the side of the wall. I looked up. Gino was climbing back down.

"Get back!" Tookie snarled. "Get back, Gino; or I swear I'll shoot you in the back. He's dead—what the hell can you do for him now?"

"I'm going down to him," Gino said.

"I'll kill you if you take another step down, you wop bastard," Tookie yelled.

Gino stopped. He turned and began to climb upward again.

His sobs spread out over the small canyon and echoed in the thin silent mountain air.

30

It was exactly four o'clock when I pulled myself up over the ledge into the safety of the cave. Gino stood on the edge staring down at the body of Marcus isolated and alone. Otto, Tookie and Sidony sprawled in the cool of the cave and sipped wine. I staggered past Gino and fell exhausted to the cave floor, pressing my body against the cool damp stone.

"How much more time do you think we've got before they hit the canyon, sweetheart?" Tookie asked Sidony.

"They should be here any minute," she said.

"We will see them," Otto said, pointing to the entrance of the canyon.

"How difficult is it from here to the top?" I asked.

"It is dangerous, but not as bad as before," Sidony replied. "But it will take another hour and a half—and they will surely be here by then—and see us."

"And we'd be pinned to the wall like sitting ducks," said Tookie. "And no way of fighting back."

"So we have an alternative," I said. "We can go now and risk getting shot—or wait until dark and take our chances on feeling our way up."

"Is there a moon tonight?"

"Full moon," Sidony said.

"We gotta make up our minds fast," Tookie said, "or we won't have no choice—and we'll have to stay here anyway."

"Let's take a vote," I said and sat up.

Gino turned away from the edge abruptly. "You go on now—I'll stay and cover your retreat."

"But that means—you won't get out of here alive," I

said.

Otto jumped up. "I for one, accept his offer—and the sooner we start moving, the better."

"Just a minute, kraut. You're pretty quick to take advantage of a guy being upset, ain't'cha?" Tookie said.

"I know what I'm doing," Gino said.

"He's dead, Gino," I said softly. "Staying here isn't going to help him."

"I'm staying," the Italian said. "If you want to go—go ahead. Stay—or do whatever you want." He turned back to the edge. "I'm going to bury him."

"Well?" Otto said jumping up. "Do we go or not?"

"We go," I said.

Sidony got up and started for the edge of the cave. Gino stopped her. "Just a minute," he said gently. "I won't need this—" He handed her his bag of money. "Have a ball—have fun and light candles for Gino and Marcus Della Vichia."

He turned to me. "Leave me one of the Thompsons and plenty of ammo. That oughta give you plenty of time and cover."

I handed over my gun and ammo. We left him all the wine and cheese and cigarettes. Sidony had remained standing at the edge of the cave holding the bag, staring at Gino. She stepped quickly to his side and kissed him. "M'sieu—M'sieu," she said, her voice unsteady.

"You would have been real good for Marcus," he said. "You coulda made him a man."

"Let's get outa here!" Tookie barked harshly. "So long, Gino."

"If you ever hit Broadway—you think about me once, eh, kid?" Gino said.

Sidony moved away and began to climb, followed by Otto and Tookie. I hung behind and waited for them to move out of earshot before stepping to Gino's side.

I told him about the whole caper, about Boyler, about the film, about my suspicions of him as a possible Judas. He listened to me calmly.

"I'm glad you told me, Duncan," he said. "I knew you were hustling for something besides dough. Wasn't any of my business. We made a straight business deal—but I'm glad you told me. It makes it easier in a way—both Marcus and myself were selfish bastards— this might make up for it."

"It does, Gino, it does," I said.

"*Arrivederci*, Duncan."

"Good-by, Gino."

I turned to the edge and began working my way upward again. Gino stood watching us from the cave. The rock was blistering hot and almost unbearable to touch. Fifteen feet from the cave I saw him for the last time. He stood near the edge, smoking and staring down at the body of Marcus.

Up over me, Sidony, Tookie and Otto continued to climb, moving very quickly. Saumur, Marcus and Gino. Dead.

Tookie and Otto alive.

Should you be lucky enough to make the top, Duncan—even with the sacrifice of Gino covering your rear. What will it be when you pull yourself up over the top. Who will stand there with a gun to your head and demand the film?

Tookie? Otto?

The sun burned my hands and sweat crawled down into my eyes. I moved on. One foot, two feet, six inches, three inches. Pull up here, step there, careful.

"Here they come!" Gino's voice billowed out into the canyon.

Slugs began to bite the rock around my back, followed a few moments later by the report and then the echo. Gino opened up with the Thompson and filled the canyon with thunder.

The slugs stopped hitting the rocks around us.

I climbed on. Two feet, one foot—grab that rock even though it's hot enough to take the skin off, grab it and pull yourself up.

I felt hands grabbing my arms. I looked up. Tookie and Otto were standing on a two-foot ledge pulling me upward.

I sank to the rock and sprawled exhausted. Above me Tookie began firing his Thompson while Otto began firing his forty-five. Gino started firing again. The slugs began to bite into the rock around us again.

There was a moment of silence. "Why have we stopped?"

Tookie answered. "A rock slide covered up the trail. She's searching for another way. Get up on your feet and start shooting!"

I pulled myself up and turned to face the canyon below me. Several hundred feet away from the base of the wall, scattered behind the cork oaks and a few rocks, they fired up at us. I got my gun out, and picking out a head bobbing from behind a tree, waited and fired. Villagers or Reds, I thought, and fired without a conscience.

Again and again Gino's Thompson opened up and was answered by Tookie's. For nearly ten minutes we fired, pinned against the wall, not really hoping to hit anything at that range, but trying to keep them from shooting back at us.

"This way!" Sidony appeared at our side and motioned us to follow.

Tookie slung the Thompson over his shoulder and took out his forty-five. Still firing at the men behind the rocks and trees below us, we moved off along the ledge.

The sun dropped behind a mountain and at once a breeze sprang up plastering our sweat-soaked clothes to our bodies.

I looked up. We were thirty-five feet from the top. Sidony was nearly there. Gino's Thompson continued to fire, loud, stuttering.

An explosion rocked the side of the wall. We clung to the ledge, pressing closer to the face of the rock. Slowly, like a giant backdraft, smoke and dirt billowed out of the cave.

"Grenade!" Otto said above me; he stopped and started to shoot.

"Keep going!" I said. "Keep moving!"

Twenty-five feet from the top and the slugs began biting into the rock with hard regularity. "Keep going, Duncan—keep going—" I breathed aloud.

A movement at the base of the wall caught my eye. I stared.

They were coming up after us. Six or eight of them beginning the climb up the side of the canyon walls.

Then, the sharp, distinctive whine of rifle shots shrieked through the air. The men below me scattered back to the oaks and rocks for cover.

"Border patrol!" Tookie yelled.

I turned my head and looked down into the canyon. A half dozen uniformed figures moved across the canyon floor, firing on the Reds, while another stood behind a rock and began examining us through his binoculars.

"This is a break for us—keep going!" I shouted.

"Hurry!"

I looked up. Sidony had reached the top. Otto was only a few feet below her.

Intense firing drew my attention back to the canyon floor.

The Reds had fanned out around the patrol and were methodically popping them off. In five minutes, the patrol was wiped out and once again more than a half dozen figures rushed to the base of the wall and started to climb.

It was growing dark quickly. The wind increased. Above me I could hear Tookie begin to cough again in the cool air.

31

I groped the last twenty feet in darkness.

I lay down, breathing hard, sucking at the cuts and broken blisters in my hand, and watched the Reds in their flashlighted activity below us. They were open and distinct in their shouts to each other. And those that were climbing up the side of the wall cursed and yelled at each other as if they were alone.

"It will be three hours—perhaps four, before they can get to the top," Sidony said. "It will be easy now to escape in the darkness."

"Gimme another few minutes sweetheart," Tookie said, gasping for breath.

He began to cough. Longer and harder than I had ever heard before. His face twisted in sudden agonizing pain. He began to vomit.

"Strike a match!" I said to Otto.

We moved back from the edge and struck a match.

Tookie's mouth was covered with blood.

He wiped his sleeve across his chin and looked at it. He grunted and began coughing again. We struck another match.

Tookie lay stretched out full on the ground, holding his stomach, head to one side, blood spurting from his mouth. "I'll be a sonofabitch," he gasped, "I—I ain't going to die alone—not in the dark. Get me up outa here."

Otto looked at me and hesitated. "Grab him under the arms," I said. "Hurry. We've got to take advantage of every minute now."

We pulled Tookie to his feet. He continued to cough. Sidony looked at us frightened, her face strained from the hours of climbing. "This way," she said and turned into the darkness.

Supporting Tookie, we stumbled after her.

A hundred feet away and we stumbled and fell. Otto cursed and fell headlong down a short, abrupt drop about six feet. He pulled himself up and returned to where I was helping Tookie back to his feet.

"You hate this, don't you, kraut?" Tookie said harshly. "You'd like to leave me here to die, wouldn't you, but you ain't got the guts to go up against the boss." He laughed and started coughing again.

The German looked at me and grabbed Tookie by the arm. Silently, we continued down the trail after Sidony, who stopped every few feet to make sure we were in back of her.

The shouts and yells of the Reds faded into the darkness and we were soon lost in the silence of the deep gully and ravine country of the Pyrenees.

The moon came up about nine and hung over our heads, skimming in and out of the mountains and clouds until early in the morning. Never once did we have to climb, the whole trail was downhill. Tookie continued to cough without pause. He tried to sip some wine, chancing that it would settle his stomach, but he erupted into a violent spasm of coughing and vomiting. He began to shake with cold and his teeth chattered.

Otto was silent. He had not said a word since Tookie had accused him of wanting to leave him and run for himself. The moon dropped for the last time and it was pitch dark again.

Once we stopped when Otto thought he had heard some noise in back of us. We stood still for nearly five minutes listening, but we didn't hear anything and continued.

Just before dawn, we broke out into a broad flat valley spotted with houses and farm buildings. Several miles away we could make out the symmetrical green foliage of grape orchards. We ducked down into the protection of the low rocks and traveled fast without stopping.

The sun caught us as we were emerging from the last of the outcropping rocks and skirting the edge of the grape orchards. The sandy floor was deep and hard to walk in. We stopped more often for rest periods now, and without being conscious of it, all four of us turned and glanced over our shoulders, watching for them.

Tookie was exhausted. He could not go another step. "I gotta sleep," he said. "I gotta. My lungs is coming apart and—"

He sank to the sand beneath a heavy overhang of grapevine and closed his eyes.

"Fifteen minutes," I said to Otto and Sidony. "Then we wake him up and go on."

I turned to Sidony who sat to one side listening to us. "How far is it to Figueras?"

"Ten—twelve kilometers. Over that high pass there." She pointed to the end of the valley.

"Can we get a car there?"

"It is a very small city. You can surely rent a cab."

"To take us to Barcelona?" I asked.

"I am sure of it."

"They will do the same thing," Otto said, glancing back toward the mountains. "But I feel we are safe now if we can get to Figueras." He turned to Sidony. "I wish to apologize, Madame, for saying the things I did—for my behavior."

"That is all right, M'sieu," Sidony replied.

I glanced at my watch. "Time to go. Wake him up."

Otto reached over and gave Tookie a gentle push. Tookie did not move. Otto pushed him again. He looked at me. Sidony stifled a scream.

"Tookie!" I crawled over to him and patted his face. I poured wine into my handkerchief and moistened his lips. The dried clots of blood on his chin would not come off.

Tookie was dead.

When I turned, Otto was untying the string holding Tookie's bag of money around the back of his belt. He held his forty-five level and pointed at me.

"This is the end of the game, Duncan. Give me the film."

32

I leaped up and stepped toward him instinctively. He backed up and swung the gun toward Sidony. "I'll kill her, Duncan, if you do not stand still. Give me the film."

"You'll have to kill me," I said.

He shrugged. "And her, too?"

Sidony stared up at me. "Please, M'sieu—" she begged me.

"Why did you wait so long," I said, stalling for time.

"I don't want to talk," he snapped. "Give me the film."

"There were a hundred places you could have killed me and taken the film—and had their protection—"

He raised his eyebrows in surprise. "You do not understand?" He laughed. "They are stupid, Duncan, as you probably know. Once the value of the film was made known to me," he shrugged, "why should I hand it over—and perhaps receive a bullet in the brain for my efforts." He shook his head. "No—now I will have the film and sell it to the highest bidder, after I decide what the secret is worth."

I looked at him. "You don't even know what it is, do you?" I gasped.

"Is it important? It is a secret men have been killed for and that money—great amounts of money—was spent like water to obtain." He smiled. "I would hate to kill you, Duncan. I've come to admire you in many respects. A little arrogant perhaps, a little too sure, but—I consider you worthy of friendship."

"Let's make a deal," I said.

"No deals. Why should I? In a few hours I will be lost in Barcelona. And with enough money to hide successfully anywhere I want until I decide it is time to open negotiations with interested parties—or should I say countries."

"We split—fifty-fifty—two heads are better than one, Otto," I said

"Give me the film."

"Was Delile—did you work for him?"

"Under duress," Otto said. "But I don't want to talk. Give me the film, Duncan."

"I told you, Otto, you'd have to kill me."

"I don't want to."

"That's the way it is," I said, shrugging. "Either you—or them." I jerked my head back toward the hills.

"By the way, you are *British* Intelligence, aren't you?" he asked.

"What difference does it make?"

"Saumur being French Intelligence, you British ..."

"You knew about Saumur?" I asked.

"Of course. He was very obvious. And when Tookie told me how you had recruited him, it was simple. Both of you were too well-trained to be common criminals. Your method and self-discipline and even your plans for holding up the villa gave you away."

"Did Delile have something on you, and force you to work for him?" I asked "Like the Le Havre deal?"

Otto nodded. "I killed an inspector of the Sûreté. Delile offered me an opportunity to escape the knife. Naturally I took it. Delile suspected you the moment you set foot in France. And when you made contact with Tookie, who was a friend of mine, it was simple to get around him. And there was only one thing of value any agent would be after. The film. When we lost them in the bordello—"

"DeJruefé!" I said. "You?"

"Not I exactly. Remember, I was a bootblack in the bordello. Delile did the actual killing of both the agent and DeJruefé. But the film was gone. An agent of Ruden's, no doubt. I am sure of it now. But time was short. Delile knew the British would send someone over to pick up the trail—and you arrived on time. Contacting Tookie made it positive. And as I said, it was easy to pump Tookie and get him to invite me into the operation. And then information came to Delile that sewed it up. Ruden."

"How?"

"One of your men, Von Walter—Delile had been watching him for some time—made contact with Ruden, then hurried to Bonn, making a rendezvous with your man there. It was simple. We knew Ruden had the film."

"How did you know?"

Otto smiled. "Three distinctly separate avenues lead to Ruden. Von Walter, who we know had set up the original contact with DeJruefé; you coming to France and recruiting Tookie to rob Ruden's villa; and a Spanish seaman, identified as a former agent when Ruden was a power in Madrid, being in the bordello the night Delile killed DeJruefé."

Otto grinned broadly. "It was a question of time. Waiting until the robbery was completed and then picking up the film, as I am doing now." His face hardened. "Give me the film."

"Did you know that Delile was killed in Paris—in the line of duty?"

"Line of what duty? That was particularly clever of you. Getting rid of him that way."

"You knew that, too?"

"Why else would you go to Paris and the next day return a more relaxed man. When I learned Delile had been killed the day you were in Paris, it was easy to see you had become wary and frightened. Quite frightened, I would say, if you took such a chance."

"You had a chance to get me and the film—right

after we were attacked by the Reds in the cars outside of Port-Vendres. Why didn't you make a move when we were being chased into the mountains?" I asked.

"You forget. I knew Delile was dead. He was the only one that could do me any harm. Why should I give something over to them—when I could take advantage of it myself. I did not expect them at the village, but I should have; they obviously were covering all our possible routes of escape."

I jumped.

I got hold of the gun and held on. He fired wildly.

I butted him with my head, catching him on the chin. Otto went down, the gun flying into the sand.

He jumped up to face me. "Now we will see, Duncan."

"We will see."

I rushed him, swung an intentional wild right and jerked back as he tried to block it. He was open in the stomach. I hit him as hard as I could. He bent over and landed in the sand, then sprang back up at me and we went down into the sand together.

33

Otto was on top of me.

He had me around the throat, my face buried in the sand. I couldn't breathe. I wanted to vomit. I wanted to fall, yet I was on the ground. I'm going to die right here, I thought.

I was free and Otto was off of me. Why would he do that? Why would he get off when—

I jumped up and ran wildly for a half dozen steps before turning around.

Otto was staggering to his feet. Sidony stood to one

side, the gun in her hand. Sidony had hit him, but not badly. Otto was up. I ran at him and kicked him in the face. He went down. I kicked him again.

He turned and tried to crawl away, but I ran alongside of him, kicking him like a dog.

Otto jumped up suddenly and staggered to face me. Then he lunged at me, getting my throat again. I jabbed both thumbs into his eyes, pushing with all my strength. He released his grip on my throat a little and I tore free. I hit him in the face and as he nearly fell back, I jumped behind him and locked his arms, lacing my fingers in back of his neck.

It was the end. I had him in a full Nelson. I tightened my arms. Otto stamped the ground and tried to throw me off his back. I hung on, applying pressure. More and more pressure. I pulled back hard, straightening my arms with the last of my strength.

His neck snapped. His head fell forward loosely on his chest and he sagged to the sand. His body quivered, his right leg twitched several times and then lay still.

I sank to the ground, my breath coming in short desperate gasps. A shadow fell across my feet. Sidony stood beside me offering me the wine. I drank a little and wiped my face.

"They are coming, M'sieu," she said and pointed back toward the hills.

I got up. A dozen of them were spread out, moving down on the orchard.

"We'll separate," I said.

"No—no—I must stay with you," she pleaded.

"We separate," I said. "I've got to get away."

I grabbed the little bags of money and shoved them into her arms. I picked up my gun and pointed it at her and shoved her toward the open plains bordering the orchard. *"Run!"*

"M'sieu," she begged. "They will—"

"Run!" And at that moment I detested nobody as much as I did a man named Duncan Reece.

She turned and ran back toward the plains and into the open. A hundred feet away she looked like a man in her boots, trousers and heavy coat, as she ran swiftly across the open sand separating the orchards.

They spotted her as soon as she hit the open and swung their line around to race after her, fanning out to cut her off. They began to shoot, half of them dropping to their knees and taking aim, shooting slowly and carefully.

She fell just short of the orchard. They raced in after her.

Sidony got up and staggered into the arbor and disappeared.

I turned and looked at Tookie and Otto. The flies were already at Tookie. I began running toward the pass leading into Figueras.

They were just entering the orchard when I started up the road toward the pass. "just a little more, Reece," I said to myself. "Just a little more."

They were closing in on me fast. I topped the rise and started downhill. Figueras baked in the hot Spanish sun. The dirty gray stones of the fortress-prison, San Fernando, dominated the small town. I ran past farmhouses and people in carts who turned to look at me.

The Reds started shooting from the top of the pass. The bullets kicked up dust around me.

I plunged into the streets of Figueras and dodged into an alley. I glanced backward. They were still coming. I pushed through men and women haggling over fly-ridden fruit and vegetables and hurried on. They wouldn't come shooting into the village. But it wasn't over yet. There would be many more days and nights of fighting against fear, of living in shadows and looking over my shoulder before I got back to Boyler, if I ever did.

I turned a corner and pushed my way into the swirling, heated, noisy market place, in among the dark faces that did not even notice me, and disappeared.

THE END

Richard Jessup Bibliography
(1925-1982)

Novels:
The Cunning and the Haunted (Gold Medal, 1954;
  reprinted as *The Young Don't Cry*, 1957)
A Rage to Die (Fawcett, 1955)
Cry Passion (Dell, 1956)
Night Boat to Paris (Dell, 1956)
The Young Don't Cry (Fawcett, 1957)
The Man in Charge (Secker, 1957)
Cheyenne Saturday (Gold Medal, 1957)
Comanche Vengeance (Gold Medal, 1957)
Long Ride West (Gold Medal, 1957)
Lowdown (Dell, 1958)
Texas Outlaw (Gold Medal, 1958)
The Deadly Duo (Dell, 1959)
Sabadilla (Gold Medal, 1960)
Chuka (Gold Medal, 1961)
Port Angelique (Fawcett, 1961)
Wolf Cop (Fawcett, 1961)
The Cincinnati Kid (Little, Brown, 1963)
The Recreation Hall (Little, Brown, 1967)
Sailor (Little, Brown, 1969)
A Quiet Voyage Home (Little, Brown, 1970)
Foxway (Little, Brown, 1971)
The Hot Blue Sea (Doubleday, 1974)
Threat (Viking, 1981)

As Richard Telfair
Wyoming Jones (Gold Medal, 1958)
Day of the Gun (Gold Medal, 1958; Wyoming Jones)
Wyoming Jones for Hire (Gold Medal, 1959)
The Secret of Apache Canyon (Gold Medal, 1959)
The Bloody Medallion (Fawcett, 1959)
The Corpse That Talked (Fawcett, 1959)
Sundance (Fawcett, 1959; based on the western TV series
  Hotel de Paree)
Scream Bloody Murder (Fawcett, 1960)
Good Luck Sucker (Fawcett, 1961)
The Slavers (Fawcett, 1961)
Target for Tonight (Dell, 1962; based on the TV series
  Danger Man)

Richard Jessup was born January 2, 1925, in Savannah, Georgia. He spent his early years in a local orphanage before running away as a merchant seaman. A voracious reader, he left the sea behind and began a career as a fulltime writer. He wrote more than 60  books, most of them paperback originals—westerns, crime novels, espionage, social dramas, sea adventures— either under his real name or as Richard Telfair. As Telfair, he wrote the Wyoming Jones western series and the Montgomery Nash spy thrillers for Gold Medal Books. Jessup's best known work, *The Cincinnati Kid* in 1964, was filmed with Steve McQueen and Ann-Margaret. His last novel, *Threat*, was published in 1981. Jessup died from cancer on October 22, 1982, in Nokomis, Florida.

BLACK GAT BOOKS offers the best in reprint crime fiction from the 1950s-1970s. New titles appear every month, and each book is sized to 4.25" x 7", just like they used to be. Collect them all.

Harry Whittington · A Haven for the Damned #1 ·
Charlie Stella · Eddie's World #2
Leigh Brackett · Stranger at Home #3
John Flagg · The Persian Cat #4
Malcolm Braly · Felony Tank #6
Vin Packer · The Girl on the Best Seller List #7
Orrie Hitt · She Got What She Wanted #8
Helen Nielsen · The Woman on the Roof #9
Lou Cameron · Angel's Flight #10
Gary Lovisi · The Affair of Lady Westcott's Lost Ruby / The Case of the Unseen Assassin #11
Arnold Hano · The Last Notch #12
Clifton Adams · Never Say No to a Killer #13
Ed Lacy · The Men From the Boys #14
Henry Kane · Frenzy of Evil #15
William Ard · You'll Get Yours #16
Bert & Dolores Hitchens · End of the Line #17
Noël Calef · Frantic #18
Ovid Demaris · The Hoods Take Over #19
Fredric Brown · Madball #20
Louis Malley · Stool Pigeon #21
Frank Kane · The Living End #22
Ferguson Findley · My Old Man's Badge #23
Paul Connolly · Tears are for Angels #24
E. P. Fenwick · Two Names for Death #25
Lorenz Heller · Dead Wrong #26
Robert Martin · Little Sister #27

Calvin Clements · Satan Takes the Helm #28
Jack Karney · Cut Me In #29
George Benet · The Hoodlums #30
Jonathan Craig · So Young, So Wicked #31
Edna Sherry · Tears for Jessie Hewitt #32
William O'Farrell · Repeat Performance #33
Marvin Albert · The Girl With No Place to Hide #34
Edward S. Aarons · Gang Rumble #35
William Fuller · Back Country #36
Robert Silverberg · The Killer #37
William R. Cox · Make My Coffin Strong #38
A. S. Fleischman · Blood Alley #39
Harold R. Daniels · The Girl in 304 #40
William H. Duhart · The Deadly Pay-Off #41
Robert Ames · Awake and Die #42
Charles Runyon · Object of Lust #43
Paul Conant - Dr. Gatskill's Blue Shoes #44
Asa Bordages - Murders in Silk #45
Darwin Teilhet - Take Me As I Am #46
Stephen Marlowe - Blonde Bait #47
Jonathan Latimer - The Fifth Grave #48
Andrew Coburn - Off Duty #49
Basil Heatter - Any Man's Girl #50
Day Keene - Acapulco G.P.O. #51
John P. Browner - Death of a Punk #52
Glenn Canary - The Trailer Park Girls #53
Jacquin Sanders - Freakshow #54
John & Ward Hawkins - The Floods of Fear #55

Stark House Press

1315 H Street, Eureka, CA 95501 (707) 498-3135
griffinskye3@sbcglobal.net   www.StarkHousePress.com
Available from your local bookstore or direct from the publisher